The Trial

Captain Cunningham was a large man with a round, pink face. He wore a white wig. Some of the powder had fallen onto his shoulders. He smiled a cold smile and asked me where I was living when the fire started.

"At an inn," I said, "near Whitehall slip."

"The fire, as you well know, started at Whitehall slip."

"I don't know where it started, sir."

He took my chin in his hand. I drew away, but he caught my arm.

"You set the fire," he said, "did you not? Tell the truth or it will go hard with you."

He wore gold rings with colored stones. The lace on his shirt front gave off a sweet odor. His hands looked pudgy, but they were strong. My arm hurt where he grasped it.

"Tell the truth."

I shook my head. "No," I said. "No."

"I am sending you back to Lambert Prison," he said. "You will be held there until you appear for trial tomorrow. And may I remind you that I have three witnesses, three women, who will testify that they saw you running about with a knife in your hand."

**Other Point paperbacks
you will enjoy:**

point

SARAH BISHOP

Scott O'Dell

SCHOLASTIC INC.
New York Toronto London Auckland Sydney

ISBN 0-590-33729-7

Copyright © 1980 by Scott O'Dell. All rights reserved. This edition is published by Scholastic Inc., 730 Broadway, New York, NY 10003, by arrangement with Houghton Mifflin Company.

12 11 10 9 8 7 6 5 4 3 2   6 7 8 9/8 0/9

Printed in the U.S.A.   01

To Elizabeth

Author's Foreword

This story is based upon the life of Sarah Bishop. Sarah was born in Midhurst, West Sussex, England. She came to the colonies shortly before the American Revolution and with her family settled on Long Island. After the battle for Brooklyn Heights and while New York City was still burning, she fled into the wilderness of northern Westchester County. There she lived on Long Pond, known to the Indians as Waccabuc.

Captain Cunningham, British Provost, who "starved the living and fed the dead" and who played an important part in Sarah's life, was tried in England after the war on charges of forgery, convicted, and sent to the gallows.

1

Someone was shooting from far away, some-where around Purdy's mill.

You would hear a whanging sound, then the bullets going overhead close. I never saw any of them, but they sounded big and mean. Father said the bullets were made in England. How he could tell they were made in England, I didn't ask. I never asked questions concerning some-thing that he was sure about. Besides, I was too scared to do much talking.

We were standing in our meadow toward dark. The meadow was planted to clover and wandered along on both sides of a clear running brook that wound down through an opening in the hills and into Wallabout Bay. There was a breeze blowing, and it made the clover look like waves on blue water.

"One man's doing the shooting," my father said. "It's Quarme. Jim Quarme. He's Purdy's new millhand. He's crazy about muskets. He got one of them yesterday. I was down at the tavern when the post came. It was in a muslin bag, tied up fancy. He opened it right before all of us, so everybody could see. In the bag was a brand-new firelock and a big box of bullets marked Salwich, England. That's how I know where the bullets come from."

"Why is Quarme shooting at us?" I asked.

"He's not shooting at us," my father said. "He's shooting in our direction. Just to remind us."

"Of what?"

"That he owns a new firelock. That he's for the revolution. That he's hot to run King George and all his men clean out of the country. And that he knows we are against the revolution and for King George."

Another bullet went over, no closer than the others, but it seemed closer. I thought it would be a good idea if we got ourselves in the house until Quarme was through shooting, but my father didn't move. He was a tall man with a gaunt face and a long, stubborn chin, which he rubbed when he was thinking hard.

He stood there rubbing his chin until the shooting stopped. Then he went off to the house without saying a word. I gathered up the clover I had cut and fed the two cows and milked one of them, Talitha. The other cow, Tabitha, my brother would milk when he got home from his work at the Lion and Lamb. They were beautiful Gloucesters, mahogany-colored with white blazes.

The last of the sun was shining level, yellow as butter, over the meadow, over the row of apple trees that someone had planted a long time ago. The trees, mostly Roxbury Russets, were heavy with fruit. Father counted on taking all of it to market, except for a few barrels to store for winter, and those I would make butter from. I wasn't much of a pie-maker nor much of a sauce-maker, either. My mother had taught me something about cooking long before she died, but I still wasn't very good at it, if you asked my brother, Chad.

The day was steaming hot, even for August; even the breeze from the sea was hot. So I started the fire in the firebox outside, where it was cooler than inside the house, and mixed up some cakes, using the fish Chad had caught, red-eared corn we had raised, and the fresh milk.

Father came in when he couldn't see to work any longer: Chad was late from the tavern.

Father was worried. "He's been coming late the last week."

"The tavern is full, Chad says, running over with travelers from everywhere."

"Mostly from Boston," Father said. "They ran Admiral Howe out of the city, clean up to Halifax, but some of the wiser ones figure that he'll return one of these days soon, this time with the whole British navy in back of him, and make mincemeat out of all the so-called patriots."

Father was bitter about the rebellion. He talked a lot about it and brooded over it when he wasn't talking. We had a drawing of King George with his crown on and a long jeweled robe. It hung on the wall above my father's bed, and every morning and evening he would stand up stiff in front of the picture and raise his hand and salute like a soldier, although he had never been one in his life nor ever planned to be.

That was up to three weeks ago, before the picture disappeared. Father blamed Chad for taking it down. When Chad said he hadn't and swore on the Bible, Father still didn't believe him. They didn't speak to each other for a whole day. Then my brother finally admitted that he had put the picture of King George in the fire.

"I've been learning things up at the tavern," Chad said. "For one thing, it's a good idea to keep your mouth shut about the feelings you have."

"A man should do what he wants in his own

4

home," Father said. "Hang a picture of the devil on the wall, if he wants to."

"If one of the patriots happened to walk in here and see a picture of King George sitting up there on the wall, it would be all over the countryside by next day noon."

"Also a man should stand up for what he thinks, not mince around."

"That's what old man Somers over in Hempstead tried to do. He called John Adams a windbag. The patriot boys heard about it and went over and burned his pigsty. They told him that unless he minded his ways, they'd come back and burn his barn."

Father gave Chad a sharp look. "You're not getting scared? You're not changing over, are you? I'm not going to wake up one morning to find you've joined the Skinners."

The Skinners were gangs of young men who went around burning people's property and wanted to hang King George from the nearest tree. I knew that Chad had several friends who belonged to the Skinners. Likewise, that he was not so strong against the rebellion as Father was. In fact, he had told me once that he didn't believe in being taxed by a king who lived thousands of miles away.

I put the fishcakes on the trestle with a bowl of tomato sauce and lit the lamp.

Father sat down and said grace. Then he said to Chad. "You're sure you are just being cautious, not changing your mind about the war?"

Chad put a whole fishcake in his mouth and was silent. The lamplight shone on his face, high cheekboned like mine, with a few freckles on both sides of his nose. I had the freckles, too, but they looked better on Chad than they did on me, Father said, and I think he was right. People always took us for brother and sister, though Chad's hair was black and mine was blond.

"No, just being sensible," Chad said, talking around the fishcake. "I'm trying to keep out of trouble with the Skinners and the rest of the patriots."

It was quiet for a while. Then from the direction of Purdy's mill came a bang, and after a moment a whistling sound, like a long sigh, passed over the house.

Chad got up and turned out the lamp and we sat in the dark.

2

Rain came pelting down for two whole days on a
   wild west wind, but early the third morning
the sky began to clear. I harnessed the bay mare
to the carryall and started off for Purdy's mill to
buy cornmeal and tell Mr. Purdy that we couldn't
pay for it until harvest time.

Mud was fetlock-deep and the stream ran from
bank to bank, so I didn't get there for almost half
an hour. Mr. Purdy had seen me on the way, for
he was waiting when I drove up to the hitching
rack. I threw him the reins and he slipped them
over the bar and gave them a cinch.

"When you were here last time," he said, "the
mare wasn't hitched up right. Backed away, she

did; ran over two whole sacks of corn. Scattered them from here to kingdom come."

Mr. Purdy had a round, pink face and he was shaped like a barrel, large in the middle and small at the top and bottom. His remembering about the spilled corn wasn't a good start for what I had to ask, so I waited until I was inside before I spoke a word.

Mr. Purdy wore a leather apron that covered most of his front and was caked with old flour, though his hands were clean and pink. He had always been friendly with me, until lately. Since early in the summer, when people began to talk about war with England and got angry with each other, he'd changed.

Mr. Purdy smiled and showed his teeth, which were worn down at the edges. "What can I do for you, Mistress Sarah?" Before I could answer he said, "I hope you're not here to ask for credit. It's twice in the last month you've been around begging."

"I'm not here to beg."

Mr. Purdy glanced at the handkerchief I held wadded up in my hand. "Maybe you have something there. A shilling or two, maybe a pound note. Let's see."

"Nothing," I answered, unfolding my empty handkerchief and clenching it up in a ball again. "But we'll pay you when our corn is ready. We have a good crop, better than last year. There are three or four ears on every stalk and eleven acres planted."

Mr. Purdy pulled on a lever, and the two flat stones stopped moving with a mournful sigh. He sidled up to the corn bin and took up a scoop.

"This should last until harvest time," he said, scooping grist into a muslin sack that had a big "P" printed on it. The sack was small, and when it was only half-full he pulled the top together and tied it up with twine. "This should do you."

"There are three of us," I said. "It won't last long."

"Three now," Mr. Purdy said, "but maybe less before long."

I was surprised. "What do you mean?"

"I mean that members of your family . . ." He paused to wipe dust from his eyes. "Your father, James Bishop, talks too much."

"I don't understand."

"He's a Tory, is what I mean, and he talks Tory. He even has a picture of King George on his wall."

"It's not there now."

"No? That's mighty good to hear," Mr. Purdy said. "But it was there for a long time. One of the patriots has seen it. Jarvis, the sweep, who cleaned your chimney."

He glanced toward the loft, where someone was walking around softly.

"Look here." He put a fatherly hand on my shoulder. "I like you, Sarah. I even like your father, stiff-necked though he is. But these are dangerous times. I and hundreds of others like me are staking our fortunes on the outcome of a war that has been forced upon us. We can't tolerate people having pictures of the King in their houses."

"I've told you about the picture."

"I know, I know. But your father talks. He got up in the meeting only last week and gave a speech on how we should put down our weapons. How we should try to reason with the British."

I was about to answer him when a streak of light came through a window high up near the roof. It blinded me for a moment; then I saw a man peering down from the loft. He had a sack of meal in his arms.

"You got mice," he yelled to Mr. Purdy.

The man was younger than he sounded at first, but he walked with a limp when he came down and set the sack at Mr. Purdy's feet.

"Ate half of it," he said, pointing to a mouse hole.

From the way he spoke I took him to be Quarme, the new millhand, the one who was

10

crazy about guns. He turned his head and looked at me.

"Vermin's everywhere these days," he said.

"That's so," Purdy said.

Quarme was thin-bodied with a scrawny neck that ended in a small, bony head. He glanced sidewise, taking me in. His eyes were deep-set and sort of wild.

The sunlight moved across the floor as he studied me with his wary eyes. It shone on the brass-ringed barrel of a new flintlock that stood behind him. I had a notion to ask him if that was the gun he had used to fire bullets over our house. But I thought better of it and picked up the meal and carried it to the wagon. Mr. Purdy took it from me and hefted it. He groaned as he laid it down on the bed.

"The sack's not that full," I said, thinking he wanted me to believe that it was. "Not full enough to make a man groan; not a strong man like you, Mr. Purdy."

He sighed and wiped his forehead. "I've been feeling weak of late. Been up the last three nights with the machinery."

"Terrible," said Quarme, following us out.

"Three nights ago," Mr. Purdy continued, "right on the stroke of twelve, the machinery stopped. Went clank, clank, and quit. I took

11

everything apart, oiled it up good, and put it back. But the same thing happened the next night. Took it all apart and put it back. Last night it happened again, the third midnight in a row."

"My father can fix whatever's wrong," I said, and regretted it as soon as I spoke the words, for Mr. Purdy's face clouded over.

"It's not the machinery that needs fixing. There's something going on that's unnatural." The miller paused. "I forgot to tell you. Last night I didn't do a thing when it stopped. At dawn, without me ever touching it once, she started up again."

"Strange," said Quarme.

"It can't be Old Lady Ryder," I said, joking, "because she's off on a trip to New York City."

Some of the people in the village of Mott's Corner still believed in witches. They thought that Mrs. Ryder, who lived by herself down by the pond with only a big black cat for company, was one of the leading witches.

"No, it's somebody who knows machinery," Mr. Purdy said. "I'll find out. I'm going to sit here tonight with a gun in my lap. At the first sign of a prowler, I'll blast away."

Mr. Purdy gave me a quick look that made me think that he believed my father was the prowler and that he wanted me to carry the warning home.

12

Under the seat was a jar of wild blackberry jam that I had planned to give Mr. Purdy as a present. But I didn't. I picked up the reins and drove away at a clip. As I slowed down for the stream, he yelled after me, "Don't forget to return the sack. It's muslin."

3

The rain had blown away by the time I got home and unloaded the half-full sack of meal that Purdy had groaned over so much. Father was at his bench in the barn, working on the grandfather clock that old Mrs. Ryder had brought in when she went across the river to New York City to visit her son.

In England, before we came to America, we had lived on a farm and raised a few sheep and planted potatoes one year and flax the next. Father was a hard worker and we always did well, until we had three bad years, one after the other. Then we fell behind in our rent and got dispossessed and had to move off the farm and into Midhurst village.

Father hired out as a handyman, fixing this and that, mending silverware and things like clocks. He liked this work, but my mother missed the farm. She complained most every night when we sat down to supper about how she hated village life.

One day she heard from our preacher, Mr. Brandon Carroll, who had gone to America and come back to do some recruiting, how land was inexpensive in a place called Long Island. And how you could grow anything on the land and how there was always a good market for what you raised because the city of New York was nearby, just across the river.

It was the seventeenth of March when she heard this news from the preacher. By the end of the month we were on a ship that was sailing for America.

Now we were farming again, and Father was doing odd jobs to make ends meet, things like fixing Old Lady Ryder's clock, until the farm earned enough to pay back the money we had borrowed.

I went in the house and brought out a bowl of fish chowder, sweet pickles I had made early in the summer, and fresh bread I had baked that morning. I told Father how Mr. Purdy's mill had stopped running at midnight three nights in a row and started up again at daylight. How in a joke I had said that it was the Old Lady Ryder who had caused the trouble.

"Mr. Purdy said that he was going to wait tonight with a gun and blast anyone he saw moving around. He looked at me sharp when he said it, as if he wanted me to carry a warning."

Father laughed. "It isn't me and it isn't Mrs. Ryder. It may be Quarme. From what I've seen, he's off in the head. He likely stops the mill at midnight and starts it up again at dawn just to keep from working the long hours that Purdy asks of his millhands."

"Likely. Mr. Purdy also sent another warning." I told my father that he didn't want to let us have credit. But more than that, he was grudging and gave us only half a sack. "He said that there were three of us now who had to eat, but later maybe there'd be less than three."

Father had a spoonful of chowder to his mouth. He put it back in the bowl and laid his spoon down. He walked over to the door and glanced toward the mill. Then he slammed the door and lit a lantern and hung it up to see by, now that he'd shut the sun out. He didn't say anything. Just stood there letting his chowder get cold and staring at the floor.

"Maybe Mr. Purdy didn't mean it," I said.

"Maybe he only means to scare you into thinking about the King the way he does."

"He means to scare me all right. He's been at it for months now, ever since the first of summer. But he hasn't, Sarah. It's the crowd that hangs around him and listens to his rantings that scares me — Hubert Hines, the surveyor; Burton, the drayman; the post rider, John Seldon, who spreads gossip like the pox from here to Boston and back. And also Birdsall. He's the worst of them."

"Mr. Purdy wanted to know why we haven't enough money to pay for a bag of meal when you do tinkering for people and get paid for it. I wonder, too, sometimes. Why we are so poor in money that I have to ask for credit every week." I grew bolder. "Perhaps you bury it in the ground somewhere."

"Perhaps I do."

I wasn't surprised. I'd had suspicions for a long time that he was hiding money.

"Been burying it since early summer," Father admitted. "Since Purdy first threatened me, and Birdsall began to ride."

"Shouldn't I know where it is, just in case?"

"No, if you knew and they came looking for it, Birdsall and his gang, then you'd be bound to tell them."

"I never would."

"You don't know what you'd do. The other day, over at Hempstead, Birdsall broke in on Seth Parsons and his wife and asked them for silverware he knew the Parsonses owned. Parsons said they'd sold it. Birdsall's men clouted him over the head and knocked him unconscious. He died two days later. Mrs. Parsons they hung up by her thumbs until she told . . ."

"No matter what, I'd never tell."

"You'd be foolish. Valuables aren't worth your life. I'm not going to say where I hid them. Nobody knows but me. And it's not money. It's silverware."

"Silverware?"

"Yes."

Father began to eat his chowder and said no more. When he was through eating, he opened the door. He stood for a long time gazing toward Purdy's mill, at the fast-running stream and the wheel turning.

Father was dark-skinned and his hair was soot-black and long. He wore it in a club tied with a leather string. He looked like an Indian. Many people took him for an Indian. Sometimes I felt that he wished he'd been born an Indian and lived in the wilderness and could travel about from place to place when the seasons changed.

He had the courage of an Indian, too; the courage to stand up to Purdy and Birdsall. He could have kept his thoughts to himself. He could have said that he hated King George. Or just kept quiet, like most of the people we knew.

4

Father ate his food and went back to work on
Mrs. Ryder's grandfather clock, which had
something wrong with its pendulum. He laid it
out on his bench and did some soldering and put
it back in the case and gave it a little nudge.

The pendulum had just begun to move when
my brother, Chad, came into the barn. With him
was a skinny young man who lived on a farm on
the other side of Purdy's mill. They both had been
drinking, from all that I could tell.

Father was strict about young men drinking, so
I was surprised that Chad would walk right in
and stand up bold in front of him, even if he had
the help of skinny David Whitlock, who was a
student and very religious.

"Good morning, Mr. Bishop," David Whitlock said.

"Good morning, Father," Chad said.

They spoke this greeting at the same time and both bowed stiffly from the waist. Now I was certain that they'd been drinking.

"Chad, why aren't you at work?" my father asked sharply. "The day's only half over."

Chad and David glanced at each other and grinned, as if they were sharing a momentous secret. Then they clutched each other like long-lost friends.

I noticed that Chad had a pamphlet in his hand that had printing on its gray, dog-eared cover, something about *Common Sense* by someone called Thomas Paine.

Father noticed the pamphlet, too. "How did you come upon that pack of windy nonsense?" he demanded.

Chad and David were still grinning. They grew serious all of a sudden.

David said, "Since you call the writing nonsense, I doubt, sir, that you have read it."

Father snorted. "I need not read it. I have heard it mouthed often enough. The colonies are English by birth. They enjoy English traditions and English law."

Young Whitlock took the pamphlet from Chad, fixed his thick, eight-sided spectacles upon his nose, and read: "We may as well assert that because a child has thrived upon milk, that it is never to have meat, or that the first twenty years of our lives is to become a precedent for the next twenty."

"But England is our parent country," my father said.

David steadied himself on his skinny legs, turned a page, and continued: "Then the more shame upon her conduct. Even brutes do not devour their young nor savages make war upon their families."

He wet his thumb, steadied himself once again. "Europe, and not England," he said, quoting Mr. Paine, "is the parent country of America. This New World has been the asylum for the persecuted lovers of civil and religious liberty from every part of Europe."

David gave the pamphlet back to Chad and said from memory, moving his arms and speaking like an orator, "Hither have they fled from every part of Europe . . . And the same tyranny which drove the first immigrants from home, pursues their descendants still."

The boys stood together in the doorway, with the hot sun pouring down, David still posing like an orator, Chad clutching his dog-eared pamphlet. They breathed out strong odors of rum.

Father's expression had not changed through

all of David Whitlock's recitations. I doubt that he had heard them. Without a word, he walked over and took the pamphlet from Chad as if he planned to read it. Instead, he tore it into pieces and threw the pieces on the floor.

Chad said nothing. He glanced at David. There was a long silence. Then David Whitlock stepped forward and gave a salute as if he were a soldier in the militia.

"Sir," he said to Father, who had gone back to his bench, "we have this day signed papers of enlistment."

"We leave tonight for Brooklyn Fort," Chad burst out.

Father put down the hammer he was getting ready to use and slowly turned around. "You what?"

"We have enlisted," Chad said. "We are soldiers in the militia, and we shall fight the King until he surrenders."

I don't think that Chad expected Father to clasp him to his bosom at this news, considering what Father had done to the pamphlet, but I am certain that he didn't expect what did happen.

"Fool that you are," Father said. He said it again and in three long strides crossed to the doorway and there fetched Chad a cuff on the ear.

My brother opened his mouth to say something, but made only a small noise. David Whitlock backed away, acting as if he thought that his turn might come next.

"You'll get more than that," Father shouted. "The King's men won't bother to box your ears. They'll fill your skin full of hot lead."

David Whitlock spoke up bravely. "The King's men are on the run, sir. They have fled from Boston. It is said that they have scurried off to Nova Scotia."

"They will be back one of these days," Father said. "And you'll be the worse for it. King George has the finest troops in the world. And the finest ships. Hundreds of ships."

There was a short silence while David Whitlock was thinking up a reply. Chad mumbled a word or two that didn't make much sense. With his long hair tumbled in his eyes and his red face, he didn't look much like a soldier. I asked if there wasn't something I could fix him to eat.

"Something to carry along, Chad. Like bread and cheese and some milk?"

He shook his head. "The army will supply me."

"More likely you'll live off the country," Father said. "Stealing goats and chickens and fruit from law-abiding farmers. Burning their barns down if they refuse, as they've been doing up in Boston and other places."

"The sergeant told me that I'd be in the commissary," Chad said. "Since I've been working in the kitchen up at the Lion and Lamb. I'll ride in a wagon stuffed with food and I'll have plenty of it to eat."

"Chances are," Father said, "that you'll not ride so much as you'll walk. And be hungry more than you're not. And freeze your tail."

Chad peered at his friend David Whitlock for help.

"We signed up for only six months," David said.

"Long enough," Father replied, "to have your skulls split. By the Hessians, probably. You've heard of them. They're professional soldiers. Mercenaries, they're called. Come from Germany. The fiercest fighters in the world."

Old Lady Ryder's clock cleared its throat and struck the hour of one.

David Whitlock glanced at the clock through his thick glasses, which made his eyes look twice as big as they really were. He grasped my brother's arm and informed him that it was past time to be on their way.

Chad was eyeing the clumsy musket that Father hunted wild fowl with. He walked over and picked it up and made a sighting on an imaginary foe.

"I need a weapon," he said. "I'll return it when my enlistment's over. If you don't mind, sir."

"I do mind," Father replied. "It will kill no mother's son in this barbarous war. Put it down."

Chad did as he was told. There were tears in his eyes. I ran into the house to get him a loaf of bread to take along, but when I came back he was gone.

I watched the boys cross the cornfield, marching like soldiers. At the stream Chad stopped and waved. I waved back. Father shouted, "We'll pray for you, son."

And we did pray right there, kneeling on the stone floor while the boys came to the rise near Purdy's mill and disappeared among the trees.

That night I lay awake and thought about Chad. I wondered if he'd had anything to eat. I'd cooked his favorite dishes, succotash and Indian pudding, for supper, and he wasn't there to eat them. I wondered, too, where he would sleep. Most likely on the ground. He had a soft mattress on his bed in the attic. It was stuffed with duck feathers.

I thought about the pamphlet that Father had torn up and thrown on the floor. I remembered some of the words David Whitlock had recited: "This New World has been the asylum for the persecuted . . ."

We had not fled from persecution, but we had been dispossessed of our farm and its belongings, our sheep, our plough, our scythe and butter churn. Still, it wasn't the King's fault that we lost everything. It was the law's fault.

I was thinking about this and why some people were rebelling against the King and some were not and some didn't care one way or the other so long as they weren't bothered. I was thinking hard when I heard an explosion. It was a musket shot. The sound came from upstream in the direction of Purdy's mill.

Next morning Clovis Stone, one of our neighbors, came by to say that Purdy had shot a cat, a big one, big as a catamount and black. The cat had somehow got away, but had left a trail of blood behind. Purdy was sure that it was the cat that had caused the mill wheel to stop every day exactly at midnight.

Then a curious thing happened. Old Lady Ryder came in that afternoon for her clock, with her hair flying every which way and her green eyes, which never looked straight at you, peering around.

It was a hot day, but she had a shawl thrown over her shoulders. When she went to pay my father for fixing the clock, the shawl fell back and I saw that she had her left hand wrapped up in a rag. Father asked her how she came to hurt herself.

"It's a sprain," she said in her wheezy voice. "Fell on a cobble over in New York."

27

It was then I noticed that there was a bloodstain on the rag she had wrapped around her hand.

I hadn't believed in witchcraft and witches since I was ten years old, but it gave me a start, nevertheless.

5

The next morning was Sunday. We usually went to church on foot, but it had rained hard in the night and the road was muddy, so we hitched our two horses to the carryall and set off. I wore my old shoes and toted the good ones to put on after we got there.

The church was two miles away, on the edge of Mott's Corner, surrounded by a grove of shagbark hickory. When we arrived, all the places among the trees were filled with wagons and tethered horses.

"A goodly number," said my father. "Come to hear the word of God, but, alas, they will hear instead the word of Caleb Cleghorn hastily thought of as he ate his morning mush."

My father didn't think much of Preacher Cleghorn. Before the war started up north, he was preaching loyalty to King George. But now that the British had been driven out of Boston and many people were against the king, he was talking in a different way. If my father had not been a religious man, he would have stayed home on Sunday and read the family Bible instead of going to hear Caleb Cleghorn preach.

While I changed to my good shoes, Father tied the horses to a shagbark tree and gave them each a nosebag to keep them contented. There were several men standing on the church steps. Among them was Ben Birdsall, who was eyeing all the people as they went in and tipping his cap to each of the ladies. He had a red face and little eyes that were sharp as a pig's. Colonel Birdsall was the leader of a mob of patriots who rode around at night, burned barns, threatened people like the Parsonses, and robbed them if they had the chance.

The first person I saw inside was Old Lady Ryder, who thanked Father again for fixing her clock. She still had her hand wrapped up. The next person I saw was Mr. Purdy, his round face pink and smiling, standing right behind her. I told him that I'd heard he had shot a black cat as big as a catamount. No sooner were the words out of my mouth than Old Lady Ryder coughed twice and whisked herself away without a sound.

There were seats down in front, but Father chose to stand up in the back. "If Caleb begins to rant," he said, "we can slip out without causing a ruction."

Caleb Cleghorn didn't rant. He spoke in a quiet voice of things that were happening in our peaceful community, the mistreatment of the Parsonses, of property burned and animals stolen.

"It is not a revolution," he said. "It is a civil war, a war among people who once were friends. Let us strive to be understanding of those who have different thoughts from ours. For we share a common speech and do worship the same all-merciful God."

I looked about for Ben Birdsall to see if he was within the reach of the preacher's voice, but in vain. I did see Jim Quarme. He was standing near the doorway, nodding his bony head in agreement with everything that was said. I felt his eyes upon me from time to time, but he was nowhere around when the services ended.

On the way out of the church my father was stopped by Master Wentworth, who taught reading and writing at Mott's Corner where I went to school in the wintertime.

"Do you plan for Sarah to enroll with us this year?" he said to Father.

"I am pondering the question," Father said.

"Why, may I be emboldened to ask, need you ponder?" Master Wentworth asked.

"Because, sir, you have become a mouthpiece for the rebellion. I question the wisdom of stuffing my daughter's head full of nonsense."

Master Wentworth had a pale, sad face. "What do you say, Sarah? Were you happy in school last year?"

I glanced at Father and hesitated, not wanting to contradict him.

"You seemed happy," Master Wentworth said.

Master Wentworth was a good teacher. If you ever made a mistake and used "mayn't I" for "may I not" or left a loose participle, he didn't make a big fuss of it. He had mentioned the war several times, but I never remembered that he took one side or the other. I liked my classmates, too.

Master Wentworth had a scant amount of hair, and the hot sun made his bald spots glisten.

"We shall miss you, Sarah, if you don't come," he said. "You were an excellent pupil."

Father was trying to stare me down, but I looked straight ahead and got up courage. "I learned much, Master Wentworth," I said. "When the crops are in, I would like to come back. That is, if Father doesn't mind."

"Good," Master Wentworth said. "I shall save a seat for you."

Father fell silent as we went down the steps. It was his way of saying that he was angry with me for having stood up against him. It seemed that most every day now there was some kind of ill feeling about the war.

Father started to say something and stopped. We had come to the big shagbark hickory where we had drawn up the wagon and tethered our horses. The traces were empty. The horses were gone.

Father swore a hair-raising oath. I had never heard him swear before. Nearby, Lem Stewart, our neighbor, was shouting, "Thieves! Thieves!" at the top of his voice. His horses were gone, too. From around the grove came other shouts.

When it was over, we found that six families had been robbed of their teams. And of the six all, but one were loyal supporters of the King. Everyone thought it was the work of Ben Birdsall, but no one was sure.

6

For two whole weeks nothing was heard about the stolen horses. Then Mr. Kinkade carted a load of early apples over to Newtown. While he was there he heard that a drover had been seen hurrying east just the day before, driving twelve horses. That was all we ever heard.

Father did not have the money for another team, but he sold some tools and managed to buy one horse, a mare. She wasn't much of a horse; she was spavined and at least as old as I. However, she could pull a wagon if it was not loaded full. No one knew her name, so I called her Samantha, because I liked the sound.

We started harvesting the corn three days after our team was stolen. It was beautiful corn, mostly four ears to the stalk, plump and the color of fresh butter. I took three half-loads to Purdy's mill and had them ground into meal. I paid Mr. Purdy what we owed and had some left for winter.

I caught only a glimpse of Quarme's bony head sticking up above a stack of barrels and his small, mean little eyes peering down at me. Mr. Purdy told me about the cat he had shot, how it had left a trail of blood behind, how afterward the mill hadn't stopped at midnight. I didn't tell him about Old Lady Ryder and her hand.

The next week we picked a few early Roxbury Russets, which always go to a good market. They are not a pretty apple, having sort of a brownish blush; but underneath the blush is a green-gold and the flesh is sweet and crisp. We also had a fine crop of Golden Russets coming on. It is a smaller apple than the Roxbury but richer to the taste.

I put up ten gallons of cider, thirty-three jugs of apple butter, and saved three small barrels to dry for winter eating. Some I sold in Mott's Corner, going from house to house because you get more money that way than if you sell them to the store.

When I was no longer tired at night, Father brought out the Bible after supper and we sat at the table and he read to me. I'd had a lot of religious instruction from the Bible since the time I was old enough to listen, so this was more to help me to speak and write properly, now that I was not going to school anymore. I had given up the idea because Father was set against it.

Father was an admirer of William Tyndale. He never got tired of talking about him. Every night he told me something new about Tyndale.

"Imagine," he said one night. It was the night Birdsall's mob came to our place. "Imagine a young man, just out of the university, who wished to translate the Bible from the Greek language, in which it was first written, into English. But he couldn't because it was against the wishes of Henry the Eighth — he is the King who had many wives and cut the heads off two of them. Because his life was in danger, Tyndale had to leave England and flee to Germany. There he translated the Bible, printed it, and smuggled it down the Rhine River into England, though the King's spies were on his trail."

My father leaned across the table. He clasped his hands. His eyes shone steady in the candle-light. I could imagine him living long ago, having the courage to do the things William Tyndale did.

"Afterward, because the King's spies were searching everywhere for him, he hid out in cellars and garrets and cocklofts. He hid for many years in fear of his life, but all the while writing words in praise of Christ. Until he was finally captured, strangled, and burned at the stake. Today, Sarah, most of the words I read to you are of Tyndale's making. Listen to Matthew:

" 'Ye have heard that it hath been said, An eye for an eye, and a tooth for a tooth: But I say unto you, That ye resist not evil: but whosoever shall smite thee on thy right cheek, turn to him the other also.'

"And this: 'Ye have heard that it hath been said, Thou shalt love thy neighbour, and hate thine enemy. But I say unto you, Love your enemies, bless them that curse you, do good to them that hate you, and pray for them which despitefully use you, and persecute you.' "

Father closed the Bible and folded his hands on the table. "It is good in stressful times to hear the music of these words. To let it echo in the heart. But the meanings are something else besides. It is terribly hard for me to remember them when I think of Quarme or Purdy or Ben Birdsall. Could it be that I am not a Christian?"

"You are a Christian," I said.

"Are you, Sarah? Can you find it in your heart to forgive Birdsall and his mob?"

"I find it hard."

Father opened the Bible again and began to read from Kings, when from far off, in the direction of Purdy's mill, we heard the sound of hoofs striking stone. Father put the Bible away. He went to the door and listened and came back and blew out the candle. The sound of hoofs came closer. From the window I saw a line of horsemen against the sky. They were riding at a trot down the winding road toward our house. I heard the horses splash through the stream.

Father took up the old musket that he used for hunting waterfowl, the one Chad had asked for. He opened the door a crack and stood listening for a moment. Then he closed the door and bolted it.

I was standing back from the window, watching. There were ten horsemen. They rode up near the barn and sat there waiting while one of them slid from the saddle and came to the door. He held a torch in his hand. By its light I recognized Ben Birdsall, his head and fat little neck thrust out.

"Open up," he said and rapped twice.

"What do you want?" Father asked.

"I want to talk," came the reply, "and I can't do it through the door."

It was dark in the room except for a thread of light where Birdsall's torch shone through. Father shouldered his musket, slid the bolt, and opened the door. I stood back of him.

Birdsall held the torch up to see better. He was not carrying a gun, but he had a nose that was turned up in such a way that you peered right into his nostrils. In the torchlight they looked like the barrels of two pistols.

"Light the candle, Sarah," my father said.

"We don't need light," Birdsall answered. He held the torch higher and waved it. "I understand that you have a picture of King George hanging on your wall."

"I did have. It is there no longer."

"That's good to hear," said Birdsall.

The cows were restless, moving around in the barn, and one of them bawled.

"You know David Whitlock, do you not?" Birdsall said.

Father nodded. "He's a friend of my son. Why do you ask?"

"Young Whitlock reported to his father, who reported to me, that you took a book belonging to said father — a book by Thomas Paine called *Common Sense* — did willfully tear this book up, and did, without proper cause, scatter the pieces about in an angry manner. Why, may I ask?" He sounded as if he were reading from a paper, like David himself.

"It was not a book," Father said in an even voice. "It was a pamphlet, and I destroyed . . ."

"One or the other, it's no matter," Birdsall broke in. "What was the reason for such high-handedness?"

"Do you ask me honestly?"

"I do."

"Well, Colonel Birdsall, my answer is that the pamphlet is a pack of lies."

I was shocked by my father's blunt words, for he gained nothing by saying them. "My brother, Chad, joined the militia," I said. "He's a patriot soldier." Father was too proud and unbending ever to say this. "Chad is off somewhere fighting now."

Birdsall said nothing. He acted as if Chad's being a soldier with the patriot militia made no difference to him. His torch began to smoke and he held it out at arm's length, but its light still glinted on his upturned nose. It still looked like two black pistol barrels pointed straight at us.

The horsemen seemed to catch a signal from Ben Birdsall for something. They began to ride around in a circle. One of them lit a torch. The man held it while it sputtered and burst into flame. Then he flung it into a haymow beside the barn. Flames leaped high and caught the barn roof and licked their way swiftly upward to the ridgepole.

I was unable to move or think. I stood there staring at the flames and screaming at Birdsall. I have no idea what I said. Then I ran past him, thinking to lead the cows out of the milking shed. I had taken no more than a dozen steps when the old mare staggered out of the barn. Her throat had been cut and she fell sprawling at my feet.

Someone seized me from behind. Others bound my arms and legs. They pulled me off, away from the barn and the house, which was now also burning. They tied me to the trunk of a tree and left. One of them was Quarme.

The house and barn and the cow shed and the pigsty were now one mass of sparks and leaping flames. I heard strange sounds, men yelling at each other and laughter. When the moon came up I worked myself free from the tree.

I heard a wagon drive away. I heard horsemen galloping off up the hill. I kept moving through the grass toward our house, which was now only smoldering. I called out with all the strength I had left.

A figure came toward me out of the leaping shadows, through the trees, across the meadow. It was like a figure you set up in the field to scare away crows. But it was not such a figure. It was my father, with his arms stretched out toward me. He was covered with tar and feathers. They looked like the same feathers that I had used to make our sleeping pillows.

7

A few people had come to see the fire burn our house and all the outbuildings. Most of them just stood around and watched, fearful of Birdsall and his gang. Only Mrs. Jessop helped us.

She was a widow woman who lived down the road, two miles away. She came toward the last with her two strapping sons, after Birdsall had gone, and they lifted Father into their wagon. She was known as a neutral, not caring much whether the patriots won or those who were loyal to the King, so she was willing to take us in. Besides, she was a Christian woman.

As we drove into the Jessops', there was only a faint glow against the sky to mark where the house had been. A wind had come up. It smelled of bitter smoke. The boys carried Father inside and laid him on the floor in front of the fireplace.

His hair hung down in dirty black strings. His nose and ears were stopped by great smears of tar. Birdsall's mob had stripped him down to his small clothes and tarred all his body, even daubed tar between his toes. Then they had strewn feathers so thick that he looked like some monstrous fowl that had come from the devil's hen coop.

Mrs. Jessop sent the boys into the cellar for a barrel of lard, which we rubbed into the tar. We used up the barrel, half of another barrel, and three big sheets, rubbing, rubbing, before Father's body began to appear. Through it all he was silent.

By the time dawn came and the sky clouded up, he was breathing only in gasps. One of the boys had gone off on horseback to fetch Mr. Laurence, the apothecary, but when he arrived, hours afterward, Father was dead.

He was buried two days later in the cemetery at Mott's Corner and I returned to the Jessops'.

A week later by myself I went back to the farm. The little shed where Father had kept his tools had not burned for some reason, but the rest — the house and barn and milking shed and sty — were all in ashes. The old horse, the pigs, the two cows, and the chickens were gray and shapeless lumps.

I didn't stay long. Nor did I try to find the silverware Father had hidden. Wherever it was, it most likely was melted down, but I didn't have the strength or the will to look.

I stayed with kind Mrs. Jessop for another week. Then I decided to go to the Lion and Lamb, where Chad had helped out in the kitchen before he enlisted, and ask for work. It was two miles west of the Jessop place, near the East River. The boys got out the wagon to give me a lift along the road and Mrs. Jessop packed me something to eat. She also gave me a Bible.

"I have three of the Holy Book," she said. "One for me and two for the boys. You take mine. You'll need it now that you'll be alone."

She got out her Bible and pressed it on me, saying, "I find the Twenty-seventh Psalm, verse five, of comfort at times like these. 'For in the time of trouble he shall hide me in his pavilion: in the secret of his tabernacle shall he hide me; he shall set me up upon a rock.' "

I thanked her for the Bible and the food, and climbed up in the wagon beside the two boys. The day was hot with restless rain clouds moving around. We went slowly up the road toward the Lion and Lamb. All the clothes I owned were on my back.

8

The tavern was owned by Mr. and Mrs. Pennywell. It sat upon a hill that overlooked the estuary that opened into the East River. It was a big white building trimmed in green and had two stories with six dormer windows. There was a wooden gold sign hanging over the door that showed a lion and a lamb lying down together under a spreading oak tree.

Mr. Pennywell had long hair and mean little eyes that were set too close together, but as things turned out he wasn't mean at all. When I told him that I was Chad Bishop's sister, he gave me a job in the kitchen right off, saying that he needed help, bad, that Chad was a fine boy, that he was sorry to hear about the farm and my father's death.

"All of the girls I've had in the last month," he said, "since the militia moved into the fort up on Brooklyn Heights, only thought about one thing, soldiers. A seedy-looking lot they are, too. No uniforms. Most without muskets. Just farm boys."

He gave me a good breakfast before I started work — eggs and ham and corncakes. Mrs. Pennywell cooked it. She had a pretty face; at least, it must have been pretty before she got fat and her nose sort of melted into pink and white folds.

"Eat up," she kept urging me when I slowed down. "You look peaked. Don't blame you. Can you bake bread? The militia boys come down here half-starved, and baked bread hits the spot. You should be able to bake real good. Cooking for your family as you've done. For two years now, isn't it?"

"I can bake," I told her.

"What do you need?"

"Indian maize, rye flour, and white flour."

"Have them all, fresh from the mill."

She bustled off and came back with three sacks. There was no special way I had to make bread, besides the equal parts of rye and cornmeal and white flour. Also you can use water, but milk is much better if you have it. Then you add salt aplenty and a gill of yeast to the quart of milk or water. Like all other bread, it should not be made so thick that you can't stir it well with your hand. I made two dozen big loaves, all the two ovens would take. They turned out well, golden-brown and bursting.

The militia boys ate the two dozen loaves in a hurry. They came trooping in from the fort late in the afternoon. There were about thirty of them. I looked for Chad and inquired, but none of the soldiers knew him. One of the boys from a village near Hempstead said that he would ask at the fort and let me know. I needed work, for I had no money, but the real reason I was here at the tavern was to find out about my brother. I could think of little else.

We were standing at the kitchen window, a big one with a dozen small panes, one of them broken and papered over.

"A bird tried to fly in. Poor thing; thought it was flying through air," Mrs. Pennywell said. "The world is full of surprises, my dear, things that seem what they ain't. We have new glass ordered, but the way things are now, there's no telling when we'll get it."

I heard the militia officers before I saw them come riding out of the dusk. The hoofs of their horses struck fire on the stone. They shouted as they galloped up to the inn. The sounds were the same ones I had heard on the night that Birdsall and his mob came to destroy our farm. Suddenly I felt pale and fearful.

"Don't mind the clatter," Mr. Pennywell said. "They're just trying to keep their spirits up."

He pointed down the hill at a stretch of water I had not noticed before. It was swarming with tall-masted ships.

"Admiral Richard Howe sailed in this morning early," he said. "There must be a hundred ships out there, lying snug up to Staten. Twice that many boats. You can see them scurrying about between the ships and the shore. They're landing soldiers, British soldiers. You can see tents going up on the island. If you look close, you will see a hundred flags flying. That's why the rebels shout and wave their hats. They're scared, but don't want anyone to know how scared they are."

I set another batch of bread to rise and carried trays into the dining room. Before I went in, Mr. Pennywell cautioned me to keep my opinions about the war entirely to myself.

"Today," he said, "we are in the hands of the rebels, who sit up there on Brooklyn Heights. Tomorrow, it may be different. We may be in the hands of the British and the fort may be full of British soldiers. Also, there is usually a spy or two loitering around, on one side or the other, with ears cocked. Remember, the Lion and Lamb is neutral."

I served the food and kept my mouth closed tight, but still I listened to what was said, hoping that my brother's name would be mentioned. I hoped in vain. I planned to ask the officers, as I had asked the soldiers, if they had ever heard of Chad Bishop and where I could find him.

9

My room was high up under the eaves. It had a small window that looked out on New York Bay. When I went up to bed that night I could see the lights of the British ships. There were hundreds of them twinkling in the dark night.

I lit a candle and read from the Psalms. I knelt down and prayed to the Lord that there would never be a battle. And if there was, that Chad would not be in it. And if he was in it, that he would not be hurt.

Drums and the far-off sound of marching feet awakened me at dawn. When I went down to the kitchen, Mr. Pennywell told me not to be alarmed.

"There'll be much drum beating and soldiers

marching," he said. "But there won't be any battles for a week or more. Perhaps not then. I hear that Benjamin Franklin is coming up from Philadelphia to talk to Sir William Howe, the British general, about making peace. Let's hope they do."

"Let's hope," I said.

There was a lot of talk that night among the officers and soldiers from Brooklyn Fort about the chances for peace. Most of them didn't want peace. They wanted to fight and sink every British ship in the bay and kill every British soldier that dared set a foot on American soil. They never seemed to think that they might be killed, too. It was curious to me that they didn't.

Mr. Pennywell said, "Young men never think about death. That's why they make good soldiers."

Not so many of them came to the tavern that day, and every day fewer and fewer came. I kept asking about Chad, asking those I had asked before and those I hadn't. Then one night at the end of the week I was serving four soldiers a bowl of Jamaica punch. One of them knew Chad by name and promised to carry word to him. I wrote out a message. I said that his father was dead and that I was at the Lion and Lamb tavern waiting for him.

51

"I'll see Chad Bishop tonight," the soldier promised me.

The next morning I woke again to the sounds of drums and marching feet. Chad did not appear that day nor the next. For a week and more the sounds of coming battles began my day. I prayed for Chad each morning when I got up and when I went to bed at night.

Early one morning Mr. Pennywell came running into the kitchen while I was making bread. He was so excited I scarcely could understand him as he spoke.

"My friend John Butler just stopped by," he said. "He tells me that the British army is on the move. Their tents over on Staten Island are still standing, but ten thousand of their men have marched all night. A battle's coming. A big one."

I pushed away the dough I was kneading. "Where? At Brooklyn Fort?"

"Likely," Mr. Pennywell said. "Everywhere around this end of Long Island."

The British struck the next morning. A thunderous roar shook the tavern windows and rattled cups.

The roar of cannon went on most of the day; that and the far-off rattle of muskets. A farmer dropped in to sell cabbages and potatoes, eager to get rid of the produce before the British soldiers raided his farm. No rebel soldiers came to

52

the tavern from Brooklyn Fort or from anywhere else.

But a few days later the British came, a half-dozen officers at first, then dozens more, until the tavern was full all day and into the night. No soldiers ever came, because it was against the rules of the British army for them to mix with the officers.

Mr. Pennywell hired two farm girls to help out in the kitchen and moved me inside to make change at the bar. Mrs. Pennywell gave me a pair of shoes with silver buckles to wear and a pink dress trimmed in white lace ruffles.

"You look like a picture," she said.

"I have seen ugly pictures," I answered.

"A pretty picture," she replied.

It was the first time I had ever been called pretty in the fifteen years of my life.

The British officers had good manners. They said "please" and "thank you, miss," and "may I bother you?" But the Hessians were different. They were very tall, fierce-looking men, and, as I found out, really had blond hair and blond mustaches, which they had blackened with black shoe polish. They bragged a great deal about how they never took prisoners, but ran them through with a single thrust of their bayonets. I hated to serve them at the bar and didn't after the first day.

The British officers smiled whenever I asked them if they knew my brother, Chad Bishop. But I kept asking, and at last one of them, Major Stirling, helped me. It happened in this way.

Since most of the officers wore wigs, Mr. Pennywell, hoping to increase his profits, turned one of his closets into a powder room, like one he'd seen in New York.

He cut a round hole in the door, big enough for a man to put his head through, and put a table in the closet and set up three candles in a holder. At five o'clock each night he moved me from the bar to the closet. I sat inside for an hour, with a comb and brush. An officer who wanted his wig fixed thrust his head through the hole, I covered his face with a cloth cone. Then I combed his wig and dusted it with sweet-smelling powder. I could do four wigs in an hour.

It was while I was powdering Major Stirling's wig that he said he would help me find my brother.

"I'll give you a note to Captain Cunningham," he said. "Cunningham is in charge of all the rebel prisoners. But there are thousands of prisoners. You'll need to be patient."

That Chad might be a prisoner had been my hope since the very first day of the battle. We had got news at the tavern that Brooklyn Fort had fallen to the British, but that most of its defenders and other soldiers around Gowanus Bay had escaped in the dark of a rainy night and fled in hundreds of boats across the river into New York. But the British had pursued them and captured the city and taken many prisoners.

Major Stirling wrote a note for me to Captain Cunningham. I thanked him for his help and put it carefully away in a packet and the packet in my dress. That night I got out the money I had hidden under the bed, the tips I had earned in the bar, and counted it. I had in British gold coins and silver, one pound and three shillings.

I looked out at the bay where British lights were shining on the water. The night was clear and windless. It smelled of the sea, but along with the sea was the dreadful smell that came in every night, the smell of dead soldiers. General Howe had not bothered to bury the patriots he had killed. Could Chad be among them, I wondered?

I got out Mrs. Jessop's Bible and read until dawn, praying on my knees at the end.

10

I set off for New York City early the next morning. Mr. Pennywell didn't want me to go because he was in bad need of my help.

"I'll lose a tidy sum," he said, "if you go running off right in the middle of the most business
we've ever had."

Mrs. Pennywell said, "This is no time for a
young girl to be traipsing around. Things are
quieter now than they have been, but who knows
when they'll start up again."

"I have a letter from Major Stirling," I said. "It
will protect me."

When they saw the letter and that I was de-
termined, they grumbled, but let me go. Mrs.

Pennywell made me a parcel of food, enough for one good meal. Mr. Pennywell hitched up his wagon, took me down to the ferry, and gave me a note to his brother, who owned the Red Lion tavern.

It was a bright and cool morning. The bay was crowded with boats going back and forth. Drums were rattling off in the distance, but they sounded friendly, as if they were celebrating good news. I followed the instructions of the ferryman, just as he gave them, for getting to Mr. Pennywell's tavern. The maple trees in the little park I went through on the way up from the ferry were beginning to turn red. I wondered if the trees at home were turning.

A sleepy-eyed girl scrubbing the steps at the Red Lion. I showed her the note I was carrying, whereupon she shouted through the open door in a screechy voice, "Someone here to see Mr. Pennywell."

After a long time a man with a white wig came to the door. I gave him the note and explained that I was seeking my brother, Chad Bishop.

"He's a rebel," I said. "He might have been captured by the British at the battle for Brooklyn. He might be a prisoner in this city. I trust you can help me to find him if he is."

Mr. Pennywell pursed his lips. I had the feeling

that he didn't want the British to think that he was connected in any way with the rebels, especially a rebel prisoner, or with me.

"I don't know where your brother's to be found," he said. "But down this street is an old sugarhouse where the British are holding prisoners." He took the girl by the arm. "Show Sarah Bishop where it is and come back. And don't talk to anyone on the way."

It was a short walk. A red brick building with three stories stood on a street that ran down to a pier and the North River. There were small windows in the front of the building and at each of them I saw faces, crowded together, peering out into the street. There wasn't a sound. The place could have been empty.

Four soldiers in red coats and white leggings were walking up and down in front of the building with muskets on their shoulders.

"That's the place," the girl blurted out and disappeared around a corner. I heard her running fast.

On the door of the building was a sign that read LAMBERT & SONS — SUGAR MERCHANTS. Two soldiers stood on each side of the doorway. By their uniforms and mustaches and long black hair I recognized them as Hessians. One opened the door for me, but didn't smile.

I walked into a small room where a young officer with thick lips sat at a table sucking at a pipe. I stood for a while with my hands folded until he looked up and asked me who I was and why I was there.

I told him my name. "I think that my brother, Chad Bishop, is a prisoner," I said and gave him the note Major Stirling had given me.

"Captain Cunningham, the Provost, is at the far end of the town," he said. "But we might just have your brother here. What is his name? I forget."

"Chad," I said.

"Chad what?"

"Chad Bishop."

There was a paper lying on his desk with a long list of names written down. He ran a finger along it.

"Bishop, Bishop. I find Barten, Barnes, Bellows, Bent. But I find no Bishop."

My heart sank.

The officer picked up another paper with a long list of names, which he read slowly, saying to himself. He stopped.

"Bishop, Chad Bishop," he said. "I was wrong. He's listed. He's here in prison. One of the first prisoners to be brought in after the battle of Brooklyn Heights."

I felt like shouting. I tried to but I made only a small, fluttering noise. I felt as if I were about to fall blindly on the floor, and I almost did.

At last I found my voice. "He's a prisoner? Truly?"

The officer gave me a painful glance. "I have just finished telling you that Chad Bishop is in this prison."

"I must talk to him."

"To do so," the officer said, "you must first get permission from Captain Cunningham. If he sees fit, he will arrange a meeting. You have a note to the captain. And I'll send a note that will help, too. I'll see that you talk to Captain Cunningham tomorrow. I'll send a messenger at once."

The officer pressed his lips gently against the stem of his pipe and blew out a puff of smoke.

"In the meanwhile," he said, "if by chance you have something in the order of a present for your brother, I'll be glad to see that he receives it. Money to buy food. A warm blanket. Winter's coming on."

I took out the money I had in the packet. I wanted to give him all of it, but something held me back. I gave him only half the money.

"Chad's very young," I said. "He has a big appetite. Maybe food would be the best."

The officer opened a drawer and put the money

away. "This will buy him extra rations for a month," he said.

He gave me instructions on how to get to the Provost. "Be there in the morning early. It may take you all day to see Captain Cunningham."

The warehouse had been quiet when I came in, but now I heard a humming sound, like the hives of tormented bees, as though hundreds of men were whispering.

The officer opened the door and bowed and I went out into the street. The air felt fresh and sweet after the stench of the warehouse. Blank faces still showed at the windows. Someone called down to me. The voice didn't belong to my brother. But Chad was a prisoner, a prisoner! That was all that mattered.

11

I hadn't eaten anything since my supper at the Lion and Lamb, so the first thing I did was to stop and consume most of the food Mrs. Pennywell had put up for me. The street was crowded with soldiers, some of whom had remarks to make. I paid no attention to them.

I didn't like Mr. Pennywell's surly brother. I was sure that if I went back it would make him uncomfortable and me as well. Instead, I looked elsewhere in the same district for a room that I could afford. It was near Whitehall slip on the fourth floor of a run-down building that seemed as if it might topple into the river at any moment. The women who took my shilling and tuppence had stringy hair and green eyes.

That night I ate the two buns I had saved and drank a mug of tea that the woman gave me. The place had a name, but the letters were mostly scaled off and all I could read was "Tal," then a gap, and the letter "o." People were running around everywhere making a noise, and I did not get to sleep until nearly midnight. I slept for only a short time.

I heard a child crying somewhere. Next, I heard someone running down the rickety stairs. The room didn't have a window, but there was a crack in the wall and through it I saw a bright light. At first I thought it was the moon coming up. When the light grew brighter I knew it wasn't the moon. I didn't think about fire for a while, not until smoke began to curl through the crack in the wall.

The place was already burning when I ran down the stairs. As I came to the landing that led down to the first floor, I saw flames leaping everywhere. There was a window beside me. I hesitated for a moment. Then I heard a voice from outside shouting for me to jump. And I went to the window and jumped.

I lay stunned on my back in a patch of weeds. Then a man set me on my feet and dragged me away from the building. A wind was blowing sparks across the sky, and soon the whole street was ablaze. There were screams and shouts and people running. I ran after them, down a dark street, not knowing where I was going. I came to a graveyard. People were clustered among the tombstones. I still held my dress in my hand. I found a bush and slipped on the dress over my chemise.

A woman who held a dog in her arms stopped sobbing to tell me that it was Trinity Church that was on fire. She had been baptized in the church and so had her husband.

"It's a terrible pity," she said. "Such a beautiful steeple; one hundred and forty feet it rises toward heaven. If only the fire brigade would come. There was no warning. The dirty rebels took all the bells when they fled."

It seemed curious that she would be worrying about the steeple at a time like this.

The steeple caught fire. Just then a fire engine pulled into the street, close to the church. Men, dozens of them, formed a line and began to pass buckets of water to each other. The last man dumped the water into a tank atop the engine, and four others standing there pumped it on the blaze.

The pumping had just started when three men with blackened faces streaked past me out of the shadows. They carried knives, long, sharp knives that glittered when light from the flames struck them. They ran swiftly down the line, slashing at the thin leather buckets. The buckets were ruined. They fell apart and spilled water all over the street and down the gutter.

One of the men dodged toward me. As he passed, he dropped his knife at my feet and quickly disappeared into the crowd. It was valuable. Not thinking, I picked it up.

I was holding on to the knife when two British soldiers grasped me by both arms and pushed me through the crowd and into a wagon that was filled with screaming women. The driver shouted at his horses. As we rumbled through a night of smoke and swirling sparks, I sat stunned and speechless.

12

The wagon hauled us through clouds of billowing smoke to a cold gray building, Captain
Cunningham's headquarters. The fire hadn't
reached this far, but behind me the sky was red
with leaping flames.

I was taken to a room, guarded by two soldiers
with bayonets. There was a thin pallet in one
corner and I lay down but didn't sleep. In the
morning they brought me a cup of tea and a piece
of moldy bread. I had finished the parcel Mrs.
Pennywell had given me, so I ate the bread and
drank the tea, which was weak. Not an hour went
by that I didn't feel the front of my dress to make
sure I had not lost Major Stirling's letter or my
money.

Late in the afternoon they came for me. They marched me down a long, bare hall, down a second hall, a third, and into the presence of Captain Cunningham himself. I could scarcely breathe from fright.

He was a large man with a round, pink face. He wore a white wig. Some of the powder had fallen onto his shoulders. He smiled a cold smile and asked me where I was living when the fire started.

"At an inn," I said, "near Whitehall slip."

"The fire, as you well know, started at Whitehall slip."

"I don't know where it started, sir. I woke up and heard shouts. Flames were leaping outside the window. I heard screams and saw people running around."

Captain Cunningham picked up a paper from his desk. "I have this message from Lieutenant Stone. You talked to him yesterday. Your name is Sarah Bishop?"

"Yes, sir."

"You asked about your brother, Chad Bishop?"

"Yes."

"Lieutenant Stone informed you that he was holding your brother there in Lambert Prison. The lieutenant made an error. Your brother is not in Lambert Prison. He is on the *Scorpion*, a prison ship anchored in Wallabout Bay.

"You thought," he said, "when you ran forth from your lodging last night and used this knife upon the fire buckets — you thought that the fire would spread to Lambert Prison. And that in the excitement your brother would have a chance to escape. You didn't know that he was not in Lambert Prison, but on a ship in Wallabout."

I began to see that Lieutenant Stone had lied. He had taken my money, knowing full well that Chad wasn't in Lambert Prison. I was glad now I had given him only half of what I owned.

Captain Cunningham took a knife from his desk. He stood up and came around the desk. He glared at me. His eyes were red-rimmed and looked like two little onions that had been boiled a while in port wine.

"This is the weapon you used," he said, thrusting the knife toward me. "Do you recognize it?"

"I didn't slash the buckets, sir. I couldn't have. I don't have the strength. It was one of the men, a man twice my size. He dropped the knife at my feet and fled into the crowd. I picked it up."

"Why?"

"I don't know, sir. I thought it was valuable, I guess."

"Preposterous!" Captain Cunningham snorted, pausing to take a pinch of snuff. "Your brother is a rebel and so you are a rebel. The more I think, the more I am convinced that it is you who set the fire in the first place."

He took my chin in his hand. I drew away, but he caught my arm.

"You set the fire," he said, "did you not? Tell the truth or it will go hard with you."

He wore gold rings with colored stones. The lace on his shirt front gave off a sweet odor. His hands looked pudgy, but they were strong. My arm hurt where he grasped it.

"Tell the truth."

I shook my head. "No," I said. "No."

Captain Cunningham went back and sat down at his desk. Quills were sticking up from a glass filled with shot, like quills on a porcupine. He picked one out, scribbled something down, and handed the paper to an orderly.

"I am sending you back to Lambert Prison," he said. "You will be held there until you appear for trial tomorrow. Between whiles I advise you to think seriously of the consequences if I find that you have lied to me. And may I remind you that I have three witnesses, three women, who will testify that they saw you running about with a knife in your hand."

The three, I was certain, were three of the women who had been hauled away with me in the wagon.

"I also have as a witness the landlady of the Talliho Inn. She is prepared to testify that she saw you running down the stairs before the fire started up in the building next door."

I said nothing. I was silent out of the fear that had seized upon me.

13

I was taken back to Lambert Prison by an orderly with a pistol in his belt. He handed me over to Lieutenant Stone and gave him the note Captain Cunningham had hastily scribbled down.

After the lieutenant had read the note he pointed to a bench and asked me to sit down. He seemed nervous. His pipe had gone out and he lit it.

"I made a mistake," he said. "I thought your brother was a prisoner of mine. I have found out that he is not. I am very sorry that I made the mistake. You may understand how this is possible, with hundreds of new prisoners coming in and going out every week."

His voice sounded friendly. I felt hopeful as I sat there on the hard bench. But hopeful about what, I couldn't have said.

"You are under arrest by Captain Cunningham's orders," the lieutenant said. "But you are now in my custody." He reached in his desk and took out the money I had given him to buy food for my brother and handed it to me. "Before I forget."

I felt mean, thinking, as I had, that he had tried to cheat me. "Thank you," I said and tried to smile.

"It is strictly against rules," the lieutenant said, "but I am going to break rules and send you over to Wallabout Bay to see your brother."

He called two orderlies, one of them a tall Hessian with a blackened face and a heavy musket fixed with a two-edged bayonet. The British orderly, who introduced himself as Sergeant McCall, was armed.

The sky hung heavy with gray clouds, but the fire seemed to be smoldering out. At the river we got out of the cart and into a boat with two men at the oars.

Wallabout Bay was a shallow notch in the Brooklyn shore, and here seven floating prisons were anchored. Once they had been ships, roaming the far oceans, I learned from Sergeant McCall, who liked to talk. Now they were listing hulks, with their masts cut down to blackened stumps.

One of the oarsmen said that this was the fourth time that day he had rowed across the river.

Sergeant McCall, who had not stopped talking, said, "Be advised, my friend, that what you refer to as a river is not a river at all. It is an estuary, an extension of the sea. A body of water subject to the vagrant will of the tides that wander back and forth, first northward then southward, from the vicinity of Staten Island to the heights of Haarlem and beyond, four times each day, summer and winter, the year round. Or so I am told and on good authority."

He smacked his lips as he spoke each word, as if he found them tasty. The oarsmen quit rowing to listen. The boat drifted for a while. I felt like shouting at them.

We passed six of the hulks before we came within reach of the *Scorpion*. The last of an angry-looking sun shone on its gray, unfriendly decks. There was a fresh breeze blowing in from the sea, but the hulk's horrible stench as we came abreast of her turned my stomach over.

"It will take a little time to make arrangements," an officer in a red coat called down. "We're badly crowded. We have twice the number we should handle. The ship's in disorder.

Come aboard, but ask the girl to wait until we find her brother and get things straightened out."

Sergeant McCall and the two oarsmen clambered up the ladder. The Hessian, who had been sitting while we crossed the river, stood up. He looked down upon me from his great height and said a few words in German, which I didn't understand. Then he said in English, "Pretty." I acted as if I still didn't understand him.

After what seemed like a long time, a young man came to the rail. He leaned down toward me. It was Chad's friend, David Whitlock, but I didn't recognize him until he spoke. His cheeks were pale and sunken to the bone. A hand as he hung it over the rail looked like a bundle of dry sticks. He had lost his eight-sided glasses. He squinted as if I were miles away. I could barely hear his voice.

"It is terrible here on the *Scorpion*," he said. "They will us to die. We sleep without blankets on bare boards. The hulk rots with disease. They feed us flour that crawls with worms."

"I have money for food," I shouted up at him.

"It will do no good," he answered. "They want us to die. They carry away a dozen dead every day. They bury them in the sea."

David coughed. He started to speak and stopped and then he spoke again. "They want us to die, Sarah. Chad is dead. He died this morning."

I had not known these words were the cruel words I feared to hear. I heard them now as if I had heard them before. I felt little, only lost, lost and alone.

14

I sat quietly in the bow of the longboat. It was night now. Lights began to show among the hulks scattered along the shore. A farmer was milking a cow in a field less than a furlong from where I sat, so close I could hear milk splashing in the pail. His lantern cast a trailing light across the dark water.

I heard Sergeant McCall tell someone that Chad Bishop had been carried away. To where? Where? To be thrown into the sea, David Whitlock had said.

I screamed with all the breath I had in my body. I screamed again. Then I felt quiet all over, as if I were dead. But I was not dead; I felt my heart beating. I heard the lapping of the waves against the boat. I saw the shore and the light from the farmer's lantern shining on the water.

The Hessian had put his musket down and was still standing in the stern of the boat, singing to himself.

I took off my shoes and tied the laces together. I kilted my dress and put the shoes in its folds. The oarsmen were starting down the ladder. The first one stopped to shout something, then the other laughed. The rope ladder creaked as the men came down. I saw Sergeant McCall standing at the rail and David Whitlock standing beside him.

Silently, I let myself over the side and struck out along the path east by the farmer's lantern. The water was so cold it took my breath. I had never swum in all my life, and I didn't swim now, but driven by fear I managed to stay afloat.

I had gone no more than a dozen yards when my feet touched bottom. I began to walk forward on a mat of thick grass. I kept the lantern in sight. Behind me I heard the oarsmen shouting. Then it was quiet and Sergeant McCall's clear voice called out, "Come back. We'll find you. You can't hide. Come back, you fool."

I took my shoes out, but I didn't take the time to put them on. I ran along the shore, away from the farmer's light. I heard the Hessian's musket go off, then the whine of a bullet near my head.

I didn't stop. I ran until my stockings were torn and my feet were cut and bleeding; then I sat down and put on my shoes.

Far off in the east I saw a small cluster of lights that I took to be a village. I found myself on a path trending in that direction, and I followed it. The moon came up, which helped me to move faster.

I reached the village about an hour later. None of the houses showed lights, so I found no one who could tell me where I was. At the last house on the street a dog ran out of the bushes and barked. A man, holding a musket, opened the front door and asked me where I was going at midnight. He came close and peered at me.

"It's no hour for a girl to be out," he said. "Where you bound, all sopping wet?"

"The Lion and Lamb tavern," I told him.

"It's a far piece from here. You'd best spend the night. Come in; we'll put you up."

"I'll be going," I said. "Just tell me the way, please."

The man showed me a path that ran off to the southeast and took me a half mile along the way. When he turned back, he wished me a safe journey and said for me not to be afraid.

"The countryside's calm," he said. "But I wish you'd stay the night."

I thanked him kindly and went on, with the

moon at my back, casting a faint moon shadow in front. Toward morning, as the first light showed in the east, I reached the Lion and the Lamb.

I went quietly around to the back of the tavern, not rousing the dog, and made myself a bed among the trees in the hickory grove. It was nearly noon, with a hot sun shining, when I woke. Mrs. Pennywell was staring down at me and asking questions.

15

Mrs. Pennywell built a fire and heated water for me in the big iron tub. I washed away the soot and mud and smoke of the journey.

I washed away everything, but the memories and my fear. I could still see the round face of Captain Cunningham leaning over me with his pale eyes and his false smile. I could hear David Whitlock croaking out the grievous words about my brother, Chad. I could still hear the sound of the musket shot as I stumbled along the shore in the dark night.

Mrs. Pennywell seemed uneasy. She kept untying and tying her apron strings. Suddenly she said, "You shouldn't have run. The King's men aren't like the rebels. Not like Birdsall and his gang."

"There's no difference."

"You're not guilty. They'll have a trial and set you free. Then you won't need to worry."

I said nothing. Everything seemed unreal. The kitchen, the crows cawing in the hickory grove, even Mrs. Pennywell herself, talking, fussing over me, were shadowy things. They were happening to someone else. Demented people, I thought, must feel this way.

I feared Captain Cunningham. Yet fear was only a small part of everything. It was anger that I felt most. Anger at the war that had caused Chad's death and my father's. Anger at the rebels and the King's men alike. And at all the needless killings.

Mr. Pennywell came out. He disagreed with his wife. "What if they have the trial and find Sarah guilty?" he asked her. "What then?"

She didn't answer.

"Best that we hide her," Mr. Pennywell said. "We have a safe place in the cellar. It's hidden many a King's man before."

"Maybe they won't come looking," his wife said.

I felt that she wished me away. I didn't blame her. "I'll be leaving," I said. This seemed to make her feel better. "I can go now."

"Nothing of the kind," Mr. Pennywell said. "They'd catch you on the road before you went a mile. If they're hunting you, that is." He told his wife to go up and get my things and bring them down. "What do the men look like?"

"One is a tall Hessian with a blackened face," I said. "The other is short and thin."

"What's he wearing?"

It was hard for me to think. "A green coat," I said, "and white trousers and green gaiters. He has a pistol that has two shiny barrels. There were three men with him. I guess they'll all be on foot, because the cart and horse are in New York."

"Not likely," Mr. Pennywell said. "You know there's a British camp near Wallabout Bay. They'll find horses to ride. Did you tell the sergeant or anyone that you live here at the Lion and Lamb?"

"I don't remember. I must have, but I forget."

"You stay in the kitchen and I'll keep an eye out. They may not come, but if they do I'll ring the ship's bell. I'll show you where to hide."

"I should leave," I said. I wanted to. But he took my arm and led me down a staircase that went from the kitchen into a cellar stored with barrels of rum. One of the barrels was empty and had a doorlike bottom that slid aside. That is, half of it did. Below this opening was a small room lined with rock.

"There's water and food," Mr. Pennywell said. "Enough to last three people for a week. We hid Judge Stillwell down there for twenty days one time. He looked like a potato sprout when he came up, but he was alive."

He put my clothes and the Bible in the empty barrel, the things his wife had brought, and gave me a blanket.

"In case," he said, "you have to stay all night."

They came near dusk through a light rain. We heard them ride into the courtyard, two men on dapper horses. Mr. Pennywell did not need to ring the ship's bell, because I saw them when they rode up the rise and recognized the Hessian and McCall in his green uniform and blond hair flying.

I went down the stairs, taking along a candle. I climbed into the barrel and slid back the trap door and waited there while the men entered the tavern. They made a lot of noise, stamping mud from their feet. I heard them talking to Mr. Pennywell, but I couldn't hear what they were saying.

They talked a long time, perhaps half an hour; then it was very quiet. I heard steps in the tap-room, which was above my head, and, a few moments later, the sound of boots striding across the kitchen floor.

I let myself through the trap door, closed it, and lit the candle. It was cold, so I put the blanket around me and waited.

Shortly a door opened and I heard steps on the cellar stairs. Sergeant McCall asked someone to bring a lantern. There was a sudden streak of light above me and the sound of quiet voices. One of the men put his boot to the empty barrel and after a moment I heard the kitchen door open and close.

The ship's clock in the taproom struck the hour of nine. I could not tell whether the men were eating supper or not. The clock struck ten. Soon afterward Mrs. Pennywell came down to tell me that Sergeant McCall had decided to stay the night.

"Don't come out until they leave in the morning," she said.

16

The candle burned itself out. I sat in the dark until the ship's clock struck midnight.

Then I slid back the trap door and gathered up my oddments Mrs. Pennywell had brought down and wrapped them in the blanket. Mr. Pennywell gave me a coin. I put the money, silver and paper, which was less than two pounds, in my dress and I climbed the stairs to the kitchen. I took a loaf of bread from the hearth and left sixpence to pay for it.

I waited in the hickory grove until dawn. Then I set off for Mrs. Jessop's to return her Bible. I walked fast, among the trees most of the time.

Mrs. Jessop saw me on the road and came running out to meet me. All the early morning clouds had rolled in from westward. Now it was raining and I was wet through.

She took me into the house, built up a fire, and helped me dry off. I told her as best I could what had happened during the time I had been away, some of the things. I thought she might want to get rid of me, the way things were, but she said she had a place for me to sleep and I could stay as long as I wanted to.

"You can't go back to the farm. People are squatting in the ruins. The Sullivans. Three brothers, black-haired and black-hearted. You'd best not go near them."

I didn't want to go back to the farm. I wanted to go as far away from the sounds of battle, the hatred and the killings, as my feet would take me. Everything was mixed up in my mind, but this I knew for certain.

I untied the bundle and took out her Bible.

"Keep it," she begged me. "Hold it close. It'll guide your steps in the paths of righteousness. It'll comfort you. It'll protect you from evil."

Her words angered me. "It did not protect my father," I burst out. "Nor did it protect my brother."

Mrs. Jessop stared at me as if I had suddenly sprouted the devil's horns. She snatched the Bible from my hands, opened it, and marked a place with a finger.

86

"Job Five, eighteen," she said. " 'He woundeth, and his hands make whole.' "

"I am not whole. I am sick and alone."

Mrs. Jessop frowned, but went on. "Job Five, seventeen. 'Behold, happy is the man whom God correcteth.' "

"I am not happy," I said. "And why should God correct me by killing my father and my brother? What of them? Why should they die for me? I don't understand."

Mrs. Jessop said, "You will understand, later, when you grow older. As Job understood." She turned several pages of the Bible, but spoke from memory, fixing her gaze upon me. " 'Then the Lord answered Job out of the whirlwind . . . Where wast thou when I laid the foundations of the earth? . . . When the morning stars sang together? . . . Hast thou entered into the springs of the sea? . . . Hast thou entered into the treasures of the snow? . . . Out of whose womb came the ice? and the hoary frost of heaven? . . . Canst thou send lightnings, that they may go, and say unto thee, Here we are?' "

Her eyes bored in upon me, two sparks of fire under her dark brows. "Like Job, you do not know all there is to know," she said. "Therefore, despise not the chastening of the Almighty."

I bit my lip, but answered her in a clear voice. "I do despise the chastening."

87

My words were barely spoken when lightning streaked across the lowering sky and a thunderclap shook the house.

Mrs. Jessop threw up her hands in horror. She plucked at the air. The Bible fell to the floor and lay there, its leaves fluttering.

"God has spoken," she cried.

A second flash of lightning flashed across the heavens. Thunder rolled, louder this time and closer. The smell of burning entered the room.

"Repent!" Mrs. Jessops croaked.

A yellow cat that was dozing on the hearth arched its back and showed its teeth. Mrs. Jessop's aunt, who had been sitting quietly near the fire, tried to rise from her chair, but slipped and fell.

"Repent thy words ere God destroys us," Mrs. Jessop cried. "Repent!"

I did not answer. Her aunt lay groaning on the floor. I gathered up my bundle and the Bible. I do not know why I took it, except that the Bible, my father's Bible, had been a part of me all the days of my life. I thanked Mrs. Jessop and fled out the door. It had stopped raining.

There was another roll of thunder. I walked fast along the road toward the farm, but when I neared it I cut off through the stubble field and came back at the stream so that I wouldn't see where our house had been.

Quarme was standing in the doorway of Purdy's mill. He was looking up at the stormy sky, his scrawny neck stretched out and his bony head raised up. He glanced at me with his wild, forest-cat eyes, but didn't let on that he saw me. Nor did I let on that I saw him.

Yet seeing him there in the doorway brought back all the bitter memories of my father's death. I couldn't get them out of my mind. Even after the mill was far behind, I kept thinking of the night that Ben Birdsall had descended upon us.

The sky cleared toward dusk. I came to some oak trees and went far back in the grove and made a small fire, using the tinder Mrs. Jessop, unbeknownst to me, had put in my bundle. I was well off the traveled road to the ferry, so I didn't worry about being seen. I ate the last of the loaf I had taken from the tavern.

Afterward I got out the Bible. By firelight I read from Matthew. I came to Chapter 5, verse 44, and read, "But I say unto you, Love your enemies, bless them that curse you, do good to them that hate you, and pray for them which despitefully use you, and persecute you."

I read aloud. The words sounded strange in the darkening grove. They hung above me and drifted away. I heard an owl speak softly. I read the verse again, leaning down to see by the dying fire.

"Love your enemies, bless them that curse you," I read.

The words sounded strange to my ears, stranger than they had before. I looked at the fire and saw my father standing at the doorway. Birdsall was holding a light, and his mob behind him was tossing a flaming torch into the dry hayloft. I saw Quarme standing beside me, tying my hands behind me.

Through the trees the stars were shining now. They looked cold and far away. I threw a stick on the fire. I said aloud from memory, "And pray for them which despitefully use you, and persecute you." But I saw before me David Whitlock leaning over the rail of the *Scorpion*, calling down to me the word of my brother's death. I heard the shot from the Hessian's musket and Sergeant McCall shouting, and his footsteps above me as I crouched in the cellar.

I got to my feet. I felt like screaming, but I read the verse again. The words were dead, cold as the stars in the heavens above.

I held the book open and carefully ripped the page from Matthew and laid it in the fire. The words stood out for a moment, black against the embers. The paper was thin. It made a small blue flame. The flame flickered and died away.

17

In the morning I took to the road again and reached the Connecticut ferry as the sun came up. The ferryman was a knobby little man with a broad smile and few teeth, dressed in a cast-off British jacket. He remembered me from the year before, when Chad and Father and I had gone across the sound to buy a brood sow. He wanted to know how my folk were. I told him that they were dead and how they had died. It made me feel better to talk. Not much, but some.

"Where're you going?" he asked as he pushed the boat away from the shore. "To White Plains?"

"Beyond."

"Beyond's a big place."

"Beyond," I said.

He glanced at me as if he thought I was not right in the head.

"Well," he said, "wherever you go, you shouldn't go alone. These are bad times." He brought me a cup of tea and a bun and disappeared, leaving me to tend the rudder. When he came back he carried a musket. "Of course, a girl like you shouldn't be traveling at all, but since you are, here's a good companion to take along."

He held out the musket.

"I got this off a British deserter. She's a little old; had her barrel trimmed off a bit at the muzzle where she wore thin. But she shoots straight. I've tried her. Good up to eighty paces and better, depending on who's shooting. Please note the butt and stock; made of the purest maple heartwood. And the wooden ramrod tipped with brass. Pretty as a plum. She's called a Brown Bess. All the British soldiers carry her into battle."

He took aim at a seagull that was hovering overhead.

"Comes with a nice brass chain, prickers, and brush for cleaning touchhole and pan."

He handed the musket over. "Take care she's primed."

I held the gun to my shoulder and sighted away at nothing. It felt heavy at first. Then I thought of how if I pressed the curled-up trigger a ball would go flying out faster than ever the eye could see. Suddenly the musket felt light in my hands.

"Everything," the ferryman said. "Brown Bess, prickers and brush, flint and patches, all for the small sum of two pounds, six. And I'll throw in a bag of powder to boot."

"I have one pound and five shillings in English money. The rest's in Continental paper."

"Let's see the paper."

I took it out and laid it in his hand.

"This five-dollar certificate for the support of the Continental troops issued in Georgia is worthless. I have a pailful of them. But I'll take the one printed in August of this year by the convention of New York, to be paid in ten Spanish-milled dollars. At some discount, of course. If you'll kindly give over the English pound, we have struck a bargain."

I had little left now of the money I'd saved at the Lion and Lamb, but I would be able to earn more as I went along. The ferryman had called the Brown Bess a "good companion." That was the way I looked at the musket now — as a companion.

"Have you ever shot a gun?" the ferryman asked.

"No."

"I'll teach you. I'll set the tiller. The breeze is light. We still have an hour before we reach shore. I'll empty her and we'll start from the beginning, one step at a time."

He glanced around for the gull. It was out of sight, so he fired into the air. He showed me how to hold the musket under my arm, pour the powder into the barrel and tamp it down.

"Gently but firm," he cautioned me. "Now you put in a patch, like this. Now place the butt against your foot. Press down with the ramrod. Now comes the ball. Good. Now a little powder in the pan. Good. You're ready to shoot."

I aimed at another log we were passing.

"Squint," he said. "You see better if you squint. And hold your breath as you pull the trigger."

To my surprise the powder exploded. It set me back on my heels. My ears rang. I had missed the log by a mile, but the ferryman patted me on the shoulder anyway.

"You'll be a sharpshooter before the year's out," he said.

We nosed up to the Connecticut shore at noon. We had passed boats going over to Long Island, but I had seen none sailing in our direction.

"If anyone comes asking for me," I said. "If they come here or over on Long Island, will you tell them that you haven't seen me?"

"Who would this be?"

"Two men. A sergeant named McCall and a Hessian. Two King's men. Sergeant McCall is wearing a green uniform."

I told him what had happened to me.

"I wouldn't worry," he said. "The British have a bloody war on their hands. They're far too busy to be running around looking for a girl."

"But you'll say you haven't seen me, if they do come?"

"I'll watch for them," the ferryman said. "Where will you be, in case?"

"I don't know where," I said and took the road that led northward in the direction of White Plains. The musket I carried on my shoulder.

18

The Golden Arrow was about fifteen miles north of the ferry. There was a lot of travel on the road, especially from Long Island and the Sound. Whenever I heard horsemen approaching from that direction, I got off the road and hid in the trees until they passed.

The tavern was owned by a Mr. Cochran. I looked for him to turn me down when I walked into the tavern and asked for work. He was playing billiards with a man in a brown wig.

"I've had experience," I told Mr. Cochran. "Over on Long Island at the Lion and Lamb."

"What kind?"

"In the kitchen. I make bread and other things."

"How are you as a table wench?"

"I do that, too. But I'd prefer to work in the kitchen."

Mr. Cochran examined me from head to toe.

"Do you wish to live on the premises?" he asked.

"Yes."

"Do you plan to stay? The last serving wench was here but a week."

"Longer," I said, but I didn't say how much longer because I didn't know.

Mr. Cochran picked up a cue and rubbed chalk on the end of it. "You can start now. Bring my friend a punch, strong on the rum. You'll find the wherewithal in the bar, which is out the door and down the hall."

I made his friend a rum punch. In fact, I made him four. Thereupon he got red in the face. He put his cue away and sat down to do a good bit of talking about how the British had driven the rebels out of New York City.

"Now they're getting ready to drive them clean out of Connecticut," he said.

He was drinking from a tall glass. In the bottom was an image of a fish. When his glass was empty, he would shout, "Fish out of water." Then I was supposed to run and fetch him another drink. I fetched him six altogether.

"I saw General Washington riding around this

morning over in White Plains," he said. "The general's getting ready to defend the town. He's got a lot of troops over there, but they're green as grass and poorly armed. The British will run them and the general out across the North River, those of them they don't kill."

White Plains was less than three miles from the tavern. That night I couldn't go to sleep, thinking about the coming battle, hearing the sounds of cannon fire and musketry and men dying. The next day I left. Mr. Cochran wanted me to stay, but I left anyway, even though he refused to give me all of what he owed.

It was now late in October. Winter was not far off. I didn't have enough money to keep me for long.

There was a wig shop in the village that had a sign in the window asking for ladies' hair, blond hair preferred. I went in and had my hair cut off. It was of a fine texture, the proprietor said, and very long, so he gave me eleven shillings besides a white mob cap trimmed with pink lace to cover my shorn head.

The day was clear and cold when I left the wig-maker's shop. The road northward was crammed with horsemen and carts and driven stock. Everyone seemed to be in a hurry.

19

That night I stayed in a run-down tavern. I shared a room with three ladies who slept together in the one bed. It cost six shillings, but mine, a pallet on the floor, cost only sixpence.

In the morning I started out at sunrise and was fortunate enough to find a ride on a cart going northward. The driver's name was Sam Goshen. He was a spare man who talked through his nose, which was very large and purplish. He wore a fringed hunting shirt belted with a rattlesnake skin.

He was driving two oxen and a wagon heaped up with odds and ends of furniture and a bundle of furs. Tied behind were two cows and a piebald horse. He overtook me not far from the tavern.

He pushed aside the shaggy, blue-eyed dog that sat beside him, and motioned for me to jump in.

He said with a grin, "Where you bound?"

If I had been truthful I would have answered, "I don't know where I'm going." Instead, I told him that I was on my way to Ridgeford.

"Friends up there?" he asked. "Relatives?"

"Some," I answered, untruthfully.

"It's a lot safer farther up than hereabouts. There'll be a battle at White Plains, sure enough. A big one. Washington's got three thousand troops all forted up behind barricades, ready to fight. And the British have more. Twice as many, I hear. Lot of them Hessians."

He took a swig of something from a jug. I guess it was Madeira because his false teeth had a darkish color, which men get from drinking that kind of wine, or that's what Mr. Pennywell told me once.

"You seem fearful," Mr. Goshen said. "You keep lookin' backward all the time. The battle won't start right off. Maybe in a day or two. By then you won't be around anywhere."

I did keep looking over my shoulder. It was silly, but I couldn't help myself.

"How far away is Ridgeford?" I asked him.

"A far piece. We could make it after nightfall if we pressed, however."

"Does it have a tavern?"

"Yes, but it costs. Two shillings a night just to sleep on the floor. Better to camp by the road and save."

The oxen were slow and the road wound upward through hills. At sunset Mr. Goshen pulled off into a clump of sycamores. I gathered my belongings and got down from the wagon. He kindled a fire, then milked one of the cows.

"Pleased to have you stay for a bite of supper," he said. "Ridgeford is most of two miles north of here."

"I'll be going," I said. "Thank you for the ride. I'll be glad to pay you what it's worth."

"Wouldn't think of takin' money, especially from a pretty girl like you." Mr. Goshen brought out a slab of bacon and cut two big slices and put them in a skillet over the fire. "You're more than welcome to stay," he said.

I thanked him again. I put the bundle on my back, the Brown Bess under my arm, and set off for the road. As I circled the fire, Mr. Goshen suddenly reached out and took hold of my arm. At first I thought it was a friendly gesture. Then I saw his eyes. In the fading light they were pink like a rabbit's.

"Sorry to see you go," he said. "It would be nice if you stayed to eat. A man hates to eat alone."

I tried to pull away.

"No use kickin' up a fuss," he said. "I don't aim to do you no harm."

I felt limp and helpless.

"No harm at all."

I tried to wrench myself free, but he grasped my other arm and pressed me hard against the wagon. I felt the steel rim of a wheel in my back. The bundle and my musket fell on the ground.

"Now, now," he whispered in a dovelike voice. His breath smelled of wine. "Calm yourself, miss."

The little blue-eyed dog began to bark.

"What's a girl doin' on the road if she don't have ideas?" Sam Goshen asked.

I tried to answer, but he interrupted me.

"Ain't right for a girl to go paradin' herself around the country," he said.

Two horsemen were riding up the road toward Ridgeford.

"Ain't right."

The little dog began to snap at my legs. Goshen gave it a kick.

The musket lay on the ground in back of him, one short step away.

"Ain't right at all," Goshen said and started to fumble with my bodice.

By chance, in doing so, he knocked my cap off. A look of surprise came over his face as he caught sight of my shaven head. He gasped.

During the brief moment he took to overcome what he saw, I lunged for the musket and grasped it by the stock. I pointed it at him. The trigger was at half-cock and I put it at full-cock. The sound came loud in the quiet dusk.

His piebald horse was tethered nearby. I untied it and put my bundle across its back and mounted. I kept the musket pointed at Goshen all the time.

"I'll leave your horse at the tavern," I said to him and rode away.

The little dog came after me, barking, but Sam Goshen stayed by the fire. There was still light far down in the west. I made good time toward Ridgeford village.

20

After I had put Goshen's horse in the stable, I found a room in the tavern. The floor was occupied by four women, so I had to sleep in bed with two others, which cost me a shilling extra. I woke up at daylight, not knowing where I was. I had the feeling that I was unable to do anything. I couldn't make up my mind about anything, even getting out of bed.

Finally, I wandered outside to the kitchen, where a fire was burning and a young Negro woman was making cookies. She had rolled out a slab of yellow dough, enough to cover the top of a table, and was stamping it out with a tin cutter — click, click, click.

She didn't look up when I came in, but went on

stamping the dough. I asked her what sort of country lay to the west.

"There's a big river over there," she said. "I crossed it two weeks ago."

"How far?"

"Twenty miles. Twenty-five. I don't know."

"What's between us and the river?"

"Between? Nothing but what's wild."

"Do people live there?"

"None that 'mounts to much, I'd say. A red Indian or two. Maybe more, but that's all I saw."

The woman put the cookies on a tray and stuffed them into the oven.

"They bake quick. Please remind me," she said. "I'll get you a breakfast."

She looked at me for the first time. She was standing on one side of the hearth and the fire-light shone full on her. She was young, younger than I had taken her for, thin with light-colored eyes and a small mouth that seemed to smile without smiling.

A description I had read before in the Lion and the Lamb tavern flashed into my mind. It read:

Negress wanted! Five feet, six inches in height, or slightly more. Twenty-two years old. Slender, two of front teeth crooked, hazel eyes, soft voice. Generous offer of 50 pounds for return of this runaway. John Clinton, Brandon Plantation, Edenton, North Carolina.

The description fit the young woman who stood looking at me. Should I tell her what I had seen or keep quiet? If I were she, would I want to know? It was possible that she did know. I thought I saw a fearful look in her eyes, and then decided that it was the firelight casting a shadow. I kept silent.

"Where you from?" she asked.

"Long Island," I said.

"You been traveling in a hurry or anything?"

"In a hurry, yes."

"I don't ask why. That's your business. Everybody's traveling these days, one reason or another. In a hurry."

I reminded her that the cookies were ready to take out of the oven. She gave me some and poured me a mug of wintergreen tea. The cookies had hickory nuts hidden in them.

She said, "Have you seen me before? You act that way."

"Never."

Her gold earrings glittered in the firelight.

"Ever read about me? You know, the notices they put on the wall sometimes. About soldiers deserting and slaves running."

"Yes. In a tavern."

"Where?"

"The Lion and Lamb on Long Island."

"That's how far?"

"A day or more by horseback and the ferry."

"That's close." She had a soft voice and a slow way of speaking. "From what you say, I guess I had better be moving. I been moving since last spring, before the cotton bloomed. I'm tired. Do you ever get tired?"

"Yes."

"So tired you could sit down and weep?"

"No, not sit down and weep," I said, thinking of Quarme and Ben Birdsall and Captain Cunningham and Sergeant McCall, the black-faced Hessian, and Sam Goshen. "I want to stand up and shoot somebody."

The woman glanced at my musket leaning against the table.

"I never was that mad," she said. "Never was."

She put the cookies in a jar, except for two, which she wrapped in a cloth. She went to a cubbyhole next to the kitchen and came out with a bundle the size of mine.

"I'll trade places," I said.

"I never felt that way," she answered. "I don't feel like trading with nobody."

I thought about the wild country she had seen. "That wilderness land, was it pretty?"

"Prettiest I ever looked at. Lakes and water running. Wild, though."

"It sounds like a place you could sit down and not be bothered."

"You wouldn't sit much, with all the work you'd need to do. But from what I saw, you won't be bothered none. Not much."

At this moment, as I stood talking to the Black girl, I made my mind up. I was sick and confused and weary of fleeing. But I was afraid to stay in the village because of British soldiers. And I really didn't want to stay here, whether they came looking for me or not. I wanted to be by myself. I would go into the land we were talking about, the wilderness land that lay between the village and the big river. I had fled far enough.

21

Across the road was a two-storied sundry shop, painted white, with a sign over the door — THOMAS MORTON & SON. With the money I had left, I purchased a long-hafted ax, a scoop of flour, some sweetening, enough salt to last, two thick blankets, and gunpowder and shot.

I caught a glimpse of a young man with a serious face peering at me from behind a pile of boxes. I guessed that he was young Mr. Morton. Old Mr. Morton had a square beard. He took hold of it with both hands and said that I must be new to Ridgeford because he had not seen me before.

"Is thee settling or passing through?"

"Passing through."

"Northward?"

I nodded, though that was not where I was going. Mr. Morton had cold eyes. They kept glancing at the musket.

"Thee will find heavy snows in the north. If thee will buy three blankets, I will make thee a bargain."

"That's all the money I have today. If you would care to trust me . . ."

"Cannot if thee is passing through."

I had the strong feeling that he wouldn't trust me even if I planned to stay in Ridgeford the rest of my life.

"I note that thee carries a musket," he said. "Ridgeford and hereabouts being peace-loving and God-fearing, I wonder why thee does."

"That is none of your business," I said.

At this rudeness Mr. Morton pulled down the corners of his mouth, but still kept his eyes on the musket. There was a sudden, loud roll of thunder.

"Thee will need protection against the storm," he said, "seeing that thee is lightly attired. I can furnish a proper garment, should thee see fit to leave thy musket for bond."

"Thank you," I said, "but I don't see fit to leave my musket."

Mr. Morton grunted. It was plain that he felt he was dealing with a mad girl. I think he half-suspected that I would up and turn the musket on him should he say more.

Rain was beating loud against the window-pane. I heard cursing in the street and a heavy wagon pull up.

"Must be Sam Goshen," Mr. Morton said. He went to the window and looked out. "It's Sam, all right. Stole himself a couple of cows on the way."

There were a few other sundries I needed, but I paid for what I had. I said good-bye and walked over to the window. Goshen was getting down to tie up his oxen. I waited behind a clothes rack until he came in. Then I bundled up and slipped out the door. I crossed the street and stood behind a clump of sumac and waited to find out if he had seen me. When he didn't come to the door, I went on.

The Negro girl was walking fast, going toward the north. We waved at each other, I holding up my musket. Farther along I stopped and glanced back, looking for Sam Goshen. He was nowhere in sight, but his little blue-eyed dog, asleep I guess when I walked past the wagon, now came slinking down the street. He eased up and circled me and growled. I paid no attention to him and went on my way.

The rain had slackened. I stood under a big maple tree and got myself ready to make a start.

When I'd come into Ridgeford I'd glimpsed the land in that direction, the wilderness the Negro girl had spoken of. It was a place where I would find good timber to build myself a lean-to, and game and wild fowl likely for the taking.

What was more, the King's men would surely lose my trail, never believing that they would find me in this wilderness country.

It began to rain again, but I started off at a good pace, though the bundle was heavy.

I passed an apple orchard where there were some windfalls lying on the ground. I picked up seven of them, ate one, and put the rest in my bodice. There was no house or barn around.

I climbed a ridge thick with pine trees and down the other side into a meadow wooded with maples that had turned red and looked like flames. As if you could stand beside them and keep yourself warm.

It was near dusk now, and, being tired and wet, I found shelter under one of these big trees. The faggots I collected were wet, but by using some of my gunpowder I got them to burn. There was a creek nearby with trout in it, which I could have caught had I remembered to buy hooks and line. But I wasn't really hungry. I was too tired to eat.

The sky cleared and stars came out, but at dawn black clouds were rolling in from the north, and a cold wind lashed the trees. This is as far as

I would go, I decided. Timber for a lean-to stood around me. I had water to drink and wood for fire. At the far end of the meadow, wild geese were feeding. Game birds were calling from the underbrush.

Around me was all that I needed. And yet I had the urge to move on, to climb the ridge that rose above me, to walk on and on, until Ridgeford village and all the villages and all their people lay far behind me.

The temptation to stay there in the meadow was strong, but at last I tied my bundle together and shouldered the musket. I started up the ridge, but as I reached the crest thunder crashed around me.

Through swirling mist I caught a glimpse, not far below me, of a dark slash in the hillside that might offer shelter. I stumbled toward it, sliding and falling and scrambling to my feet. The opening, I found to my surprise, was the mouth of a cave that ran back into the hill.

I stopped and peered inside. I heard loud breathing, the sound of things moving about, then the clack of hoofs against rock. I took a step farther and shouted.

Echoes wandered back to me. There was a moment of silence. Then a rush of air and hurtling bodies and a living stream burst forth from the cave, swept past me, and was lost in the mist. I had routed a herd of deer that had taken shelter from the storm.

Sounds still came from the cave. I ventured another step and shouted again. I crept farther and saw dimly a pair of foxes standing in a corner of the cave, staring at me in fright. I routed them out and down the hillside.

It was hard to see far into the cave, but near the entrance I found a scattering of wood that someone had left. Using powder and my tinderbox, I started a fire.

I sat down by the fire and laid the musket beside me. I ate the rest of the windfall apples I had gathered. I listened to the sound of the north wind and the rain lashing the trees. The fire made warm shadows on the dark stone.

"At last I have found a place to rest," I said. I was tempted to pray but didn't.

22

The day was dawning cold and clear. Its first light shone through the jagged mouth of the cave. I gazed around me at what I had only dimly seen before.

I was in a room shaped like an irregular square, with smooth walls and a stone floor. The walls slanted inward and came together high over my head to form a crude vault. At the top of this vault was a jagged hole that let in the light.

In the center of the room, near the place where I had built a fire, was a ring of ashes, and beside it sat six clay pots, all of them broken. On the four walls were pictures painted in dim red and brown colors, showing a bear, a large forest cat of some sort, and a herd of running deer.

At first, gazing around me, I felt uncomfortable. People had lived here once. The ashes were cold and the pots covered with dust, yet the people might return. But as I sat there I began to feel differently about them, whoever they were, those who had built fires and painted pictures. Their pictures had almost faded away into the stone. Their pots were broken. Their fires were rings of cold gray ashes. The cave had been here for a long, long time. Likely it had sheltered many. It had sheltered those who had been here last, and they in turn had left.

I got to my feet. The fire was dying. I kindled it with powder and rolled a big log up against it. It was then, when the fire began to burn anew, that I decided. I had gone far. I had gone far enough.

I went to the mouth of the cave and looked out. The sun was behind a ridge. It was the dark time before the real dawn. Below me, at the foot of a wooded slope, were two small ponds and between them a deep blue lake that stretched away to the west. It was a beautiful land that lay there in the shadows before dawn.

"Yes," I said to myself, "I have gone as far as I will go."

While I stood at the mouth of the cave, gazing down at the wilderness of forest and water, I was aware of a rushing sound, softer than the running deer had made, but loud. It was the sound of wings, of hundreds of wings pouring past me into the mouth of the cave.

The flight lasted for several minutes. When it was over I went back into the cave. At the very top of the vault was a gleam of sunlight. It shone on a black, heaving mass of twittering bats hanging upside down from a rocky ledge.

I couldn't live in a cave full of noisy creatures, so the first thing I did was to build a lean-to outside against the face of a rock. That took me a half-morning of hard work.

I remembered that one summer at home we had a pair of bats fly into the house. They stayed there, hanging on a rafter for three days, until Father thought of leaving a door open at night. "They flew in at night," he said; "they'll leave the same time." And they did.

At dusk, after the bats had flown out, some from the opening at the top, but most of them from below, swooping past by the hundreds but never touching me, I covered the mouth of the cave with a blanket. The opening at the top I left to serve as a smoke hole.

The next morning I saw some of the creatures hanging upside down in the trees around the cave. The following day I saw none. They apparently had found a new home somewhere. I gathered pine wood and built a big fire in the cave and kept it going for two days.

At the end of that time I collected my belongings and left the lean-to. I was happy to learn that the pine smoke had cleaned out the heavy air. I needed the blanket at night, so I took it down and made a crude hingeless door of birch saplings.

Near the mouth of the cave, in the midst of an alder grove, three springs came out of the rocks and formed a stream that wandered down the slope and emptied into the lake. There were many pools along the way, some dammed up by beavers, all with fish. I caught two small trout by chasing them into the shallows and scooping them out on the bank.

I cooked both for supper, being hungry for the first time in weeks. A cold wind was blowing, and I thought that what I heard was the wind whistling through the cracks in my makeshift door. Then I caught glimpses of a shadowy figure darting back and forth. It would disappear high up toward the roof. Then it would fly toward the door.

I remembered again the time that the two bats flew into our house. The first night I got scared and hid in the woodshed. While I was hiding, my brother, Chad, rolled up one of my stockings. He came to the door and shouted that bats were flying. At the same moment he threw the rolled-up stocking and hit me square on the head. I thought it was one of the bats and that it was tangled in my hair. I jumped up and screamed and ran outside.

I thought about that time now as the bat swooped around my ears. At last I got up and took down the door. In a second it was gone. At dawn when I went out it was clinging to one of the birch saplings. It was smaller than my hand and pure white, except for a pink dot on its forehead and small, pink markings under its wings. I carried the bat inside and put it in a dark corner. At dusk I took down the door and it flew off to hunt for food. At dawn it returned.

I thought hard, trying to find a name for the little creature.

23

There was so much I had to do that the following day I got in a panic and did nothing except sit in front of the cave and watch the flocks of geese flying down from the north. They circled the lake in wedges, calling and honking, then settled on the lake. Some of the flocks flew close, and I could see their black, shining necks and the white slashes on their cheeks.

But the next day I worked hard gathering acorns, about three bushels of them, which I husked, then pounded with a rock and washed in the stream. I spread the coarse flour on a blanket in front of the fire and let it dry all night. Using part of a hollow log and a club, I ground the flour still further. That night I set it out to dry again.

There were many dried gourds in the meadow. I cleaned out a dozen of the biggest and filled them with flour. I made a big loaf of bread for supper. It was much coarser and not so flavorful as the wheat flour from Purdy's mill, but better than it might have been.

The weather continued bright and cold. The maples were still aflame. Geese kept coming in from the north, so many that they shaded the sun, so many that I managed to kill two of them with only one shot. The feathers I stuffed between the two blankets, which made a thick, warm comforter. I made a bed of pine boughs laced with moss and rushes. It was not so soft as my bed at home nor some of the beds I had slept in during my travels. But I was tired out every night and could have slept on the bare stone.

For five days I brought in firewood from the surrounding forest. I cut some, but mostly it was timber that had fallen during storms in years past. It made a stack that filled one whole side of the cave, a row deep and shoulder high. It was enough, I knew from times on the farm, to keep a fire burning through the long days and nights of winter, with some to spare.

I still lacked meat. I had seen tracks along the edge of the marsh where a bear had been feeding, but I had strong doubts about my skill with the musket, despite my lucky shot at the geese. I

121

had threatened Sam Goshen with it. But I had not confronted a bear. My brother had killed one, a small one, but remembering the scare he had had with it, I decided against the idea. If I came upon a bear suddenly and had a choice of shooting or being clawed, that would be different.

Herds of deer came down to the pond every evening to drink, about a dozen of them in each herd, plump and sleek after summer feeding. On the farm my brother shot deer all year long, and I had helped him dress the carcasses. I cooked and ate the meat. But I never enjoyed any of it. I remembered how beautiful their eyes were when they were living.

I killed one of them and had no bad feelings about it. I stretched the hide and pegged it out to dry in front of the cave. I planned to make a mat from part of it and a bedcover from the rest. The first night, however, animals came — I think they were foxes — and dragged the hide away. I found the hide, but it was so chewed-up I could not use it, though I did save some strips.

I fished in the stream and caught trout. They were so plentiful that I had no trouble scooping them out of the shallows and onto the bank.

They had many colored speckles and their flesh was pink. I split them down the center and cooked them crisp over the fire, heads and all. I thought about smoking some for winter, but put it off from day to day. There were too many things to do.

I made wicks from threads I stole from the blankets, poured deer tallow in more than a dozen dry gourds, and made candles that would burn for days, each of them. I also made a store of rush lights, using deer tallow and rushes gathered in the marsh.

If I'd had flax or wool, I might have tried to fashion a small loom, for I needed a dress badly. As it was, I had nothing to do after supper except go to bed. I had no desire to read the Bible. I had put it away on a shelf I made when I first came and had not taken it down.

The white bat was company. I let it out at dusk every night and watched it fly away. Sometimes it would fly around the mouth of the cave while I stood there, as if it did so to be friendly. I still had not thought of a name for it.

I lost track of the days. It was November, but I could not account for all the time since I had left the Lion and Lamb. Guessing, I decided the date was November seventh. I scratched it on the wall with my jackknife. It was as good a date as any. Thereafter, I would scratch a mark beside it, one for each day that passed.

24

The wind blew hard that night. It rattled the makeshift door and made strange noises high up in the ceiling. At dawn it died away. Everything was so quiet that I decided that snow must be falling. Then I heard sounds again and I thought that it was an animal scratching around. But when I went outside a man was standing not a dozen paces away.

There was a low-growing bush between us, so I saw his face before I saw the rest of him. It was an Indian face, dark and long, with black eyes that caught the dawnlight. He peered at me in surprise, as if he had come unexpectedly upon an animal he had been stalking.

The Indian — he was neither young nor old

— moved from behind the bush. He held up his hands to show that he was not armed. In response to this friendly gesture I leaned my musket against the wall. Only then did I see that he had a hunting knife tucked into the top of one of his buckskin leggings.

He touched himself on the chest and spoke a long word that I took to be his name. It sounded like Wantiticut. He wore a greasy deerskin jacket hung with tiny pieces of copper. From it he drew forth a sheet of paper, which he unfolded and thrust toward me.

The paper was greasy from much handling and most of the writing was blurred, but I made out the words "White Plains" and the name "Yellow Monkey Tavern."

The Indian held the paper in front of me for only a moment. Before I had a chance to read further, he thrust it back in his jacket. At the same time, he made a gesture that took in the ponds, the lake, the stream, the forest, all the country that lay around us.

"Mine," he said in a haughty voice. "Mine."

The ax was propped against a tree that I planned to cut down for a new door frame. The Indian strode over and lifted it to his shoulder. He glanced around, searching to see if I had anything else that suited his fancy. His eyes fastened on the white bat, which had returned from its nightly wanderings and was hanging above the door.

"No good," he said and raised the ax to crush it.

I stepped in front of him and put the bat inside the cave.

Again he shook the paper in my face and made a gesture that took in everything within his sight.

"Mine," he repeated. "Waccabuc, mine."

I was fairly sure that the paper had nothing to do with me. Most likely he had picked it up somewhere in his wanderings and was trying to pass it off as a deed of ownership.

The Indian stared at me and waited. I wanted to tell him that I owned nothing, not the meadow, not the lake, not the trees, not the cave.

We stared at each other in silence. His eyes were hard, like the glint of the knife tucked away in his legging.

I wanted to tell him that, though I laid no claim to what lay around us, I would not leave it. I had come here from a far distance, and I was not to be driven out by him nor by anyone.

He looked from me to the musket. It was standing near at hand. I picked it up and pointed to the ax he held on his shoulder. He made no move to put it down, but grunted in an insolent way. He then glanced about, apparently for something else to take.

126

I half-cocked the trigger. It caused a small noise in the quiet morning. I pointed to the ax and said the word he had used and knew. "Mine."

He moved his feet at the click of the trigger. His eyes shifted in my direction and in them was a hard light. I expected him to lunge forward at any moment and use the ax upon me. I cocked the trigger. It made a loud sound. I raised the musket and pointed it at him again. I told him once more that the ax belonged to me.

He hesitated with his mouth open. Then he said something in his own language, dropped the ax on the ground, and made his way down the slope, along the stream to the edge of the pond. His canoe was pulled up on shore. He lifted it into the water and sped away, using his paddle on one side, then the other.

I watched until he was out of sight. The rest of the day I looked for him, thinking that he might return. That night I lay awake, the musket at my side.

25

Signs were everywhere of a long winter to come — the same deep ice and snow we'd had two years before at home.

Tree squirrels gathered nuts at a frantic rate, scarcely pausing in their labors. The flying squirrels, which are usually nocturnal, were out at dusk gathering the last of the hickory nuts, blown down by two days of wind. Their undersides were a sparkling white and heavily furred, a certain sign, my father had said, of early snow. The wild geese began their journey south, even leaving the lake at night, until one cold morning it was deserted. I missed the cries and the shining wedges.

After three wild misses and waste of powder

and ball, I shot another deer and smoked the meat. I dipped a dozen candles from the tallow and two dozen rush lights from rushes I gathered along the two ponds. Then I began on a door for the cave. The rush lights and candles were easy tasks, because I had made them at home many times before. But the door caused me trouble.

First, the opening to the cave was jagged on both sides and at the top. With my ax I cut out a frame to fit, and then chinked the holes between the rock and the wood with mud mixed with straw. This was the easy part. The hard part came when I tried to make the door itself.

I had no tools except the ax and the jackknife. The knife had belonged to my father, and I had it saved from the burning. Although I had never made anything out of wood before, if I'd had proper tools I could have managed something.

I cut out rough boards to fit the door frame, but without an auger I had no way of boring holes for the cross pieces. Instead, I bound them together with leather thongs. Then I had to push the rough door into place. It still was not a door, because it lacked hinges. Finally, I gave up and just leaned it against the opening. It covered half of it, that was all. I could squeeze inside, but so could the cold. Then two days after I set it up, a hard wind came and blew it down.

Except for the door I was fairly snug against

the winter, even a deep winter, but I would have little to do after supper. I had neither flax nor wool nor the means to weave them. At the farm I had always stayed up, working long after the men were in bed.

I thought about making a journey into Ridgeford village to buy needle and thread and cloth for a dress. I had less than ten shillings to my name, but possibly I could earn money at the inn.

I thought about this for several days. The trees were bare, as well as most of the bushes, which would make traveling easier. But I was afraid to go. Captain Cunningham's men most likely would not be there looking, but they might be. The truth was, I didn't want to see anyone.

I had been so busy gathering wood and food, I had neglected the cave. It looked like a bear's nest, things stuck here and there underfoot. I spent a day cleaning up. I made a broom out of marsh rushes and swept up the stone floor and covered it with tallow, which made it shine in the firelight.

While I was sweeping a strange thing happened. The broom had a long handle, and I was flailing away at the dirt when the white bat started to fly. Night was falling, the time it always went out on its night journeys. Suddenly it began to swoop back and forth around me, darting in and out, squeaking as it went.

I marveled that it didn't touch the swinging broom. Suddenly, the thought struck me that it was playing a game, seeing how close it could come without colliding. I swept faster. I swung the broom around my head. The bat flew in and out; I swung faster and faster. The bat still whizzed in and out.

Exhausted by the game, I finally let the little creature fly away. I had the feeling that if bats could laugh, this one was laughing now as it disappeared in the dusk.

That night I gave it a name. The creature was white, which made me think of angels. I thought of all the angels I could remember — the blessed angels, Raphael, Chamuel, Michael, Uriel, Jophiel, Zadkiel, and Gabriel. I thought of the Throne Angels and the Angel Rulers of the Seven Heavens and the Angels of the Twelve Months of the Year, the Angels of the Hours of the Day and Night, all I could think of.

Remembering the creature's wide mouth and long, pointed teeth, I thought of Isaiah 14 and Lucifer, the fallen angel. But at last I named it after the Archangel Gabriel. Gabriel of Waccabuc.

26

On the morning of the nineteenth of November — at least this was the date I scratched on my calendar — a north wind brought a dusting of snow. It stayed on the ground only until nightfall, but the wind kept up and was piercing cold.

The last day of the wind visitors came — a young man and his wife, with a baby strapped to her back, and a child holding her hand. At first sight I took her to be an Indian, with her high cheekbones and coppery skin. But then I saw that she had blue eyes and was only part Indian. She spoke with an accent, but I understood her.

"My name is Helen," she said. "And this is my husband, John Longknife. My little girl is named Bertha. The baby has no name yet. We are waiting for a better moon. Then we will give her a name."

The young man seemed ill at ease. I took it that stopping by for a visit was his wife's idea. I had things to do, but I opened the door and invited them in.

We sat around the fire. Mrs. Longknife took off her shoes and warmed her feet. Her husband kept his shoes on.

"We come in the summertime and fish in the lake," the woman said. "We fished here last summer. We caught more than a hundred trout. That was before you came."

I asked her where she lived.

She pointed north. "Over the ridge, a day's journey in the summer, longer in the winter," she said. "My grandfather lived here at nearby Waccabuc, which is the Indian name for Long Pond. He lived here before the time the white men burned a hundred tents in the village beyond Ridgeford and killed almost two hundred Indians. All of them. He owned the land around the lake. But he sold it to a white man for a barrel of something to drink. The man's name was Tibbets. Is that your name, Tibbets?"

"No, it's Sarah Bishop."

She glanced at her husband, but nothing passed between them that I could see. I wondered if she was going to lay claim to the land, as the Indian Wantiticut had done.

"You are a granddaughter, maybe," the girl said.

"Maybe," I answered and asked her if she would like to drink some tea.

Her husband said, "Good."

He was a handsome young man with strong features and a soft voice.

I put water on the fire to heat. I still wondered why they had come. If they had come to claim the land, what could I do? I would run them off with the musket, as I had Wantiticut, I decided.

They spoke together in their own tongue while I was making the tea. They drank the tea with wry faces, but tried not to let me see that they didn't like it. The girl wanted to know what it was.

"Wintergreen," I said.

"There is another tea," she told me. "You have the berries growing here. I have seen them by the lake. I will help you gather them sometime."

My heart, which had been thumping, settled down.

The young man said, "You have canoe?"

"No."

"You want?"

"Yes." I lived on a big lake and could use a canoe. "Someday I'll need one."

134

"Good. We fix him someday."

He spoke to his wife, using Indian words, which she translated.

"My husband says that it will take a long time to gather bark for a canoe and, besides, the season is not good for gathering. He will help you in the spring. Now he will show you how to make a dugout. It will be of use when you go out to fish in the lake where the fish are big."

"I'll not need one this winter," I said.

"Winter is long," she answered. "I know from the winters I have lived. It will keep your hands busy, making a dugout."

"We go," said her husband. "For dugout."

Above the cave was a small stand of pine. He selected the largest of the trees, and, spelling each other, we felled it. He sharpened the ax on a stone and we cut a piece twelve feet long from the trunk. It was much too heavy to carry, even for the three of us, so we rolled it down the hill and inched it into the cave. It took all that day.

John Longknife hollowed out a shallow place on top of the log and into it poured hot coals that took hold at once.

"There is much more for him to tell you," his wife said. "He will show you in the morning how the log is hollowed out."

They had smoked trout with them and I made a pot of gruel and more tea. We sat around the fire and ate, while the log slowly burned. From time to time John Longknife got up and chopped a path for the fire to take.

I wanted them to sleep in the cave, but they put up a shelter outside. In the morning, after we had eaten, the young Indian showed me how the fire must burn. He drew a line along the top of the log with my jackknife and curves front and back to mark the bow and stern.

He spoke to his wife and she said, "The fire must not burn too far. The burning must stop when the shell is twice as thick as your hand. Then you use the ax to cut it down some more. Until the sides are no thicker than your hand, except for the bottom. The bottom must be left deeper. You must use wet clay to guide the fire."

Her husband held his hands apart to show how deep the bottom must be.

Then the Longknifes left their children with me and went down to the lake and fished the rest of the morning. They came back with dozens of fat trout, much bigger than those I caught in the stream. They built a hickory fire against the face of the cave and smoked them, taking the rest of the afternoon and that night.

In the morning the ground was covered with frost. John Longknife looked up at the gray sky and said that winter would come soon. "Two days maybe."

Helen Longknife nodded. "My husband knows the signs. Do you have snowshoes for the winter?"

"No."

"You will need them when you travel."

"I don't plan to travel."

"You can get sick. You are a long way from the village. You are alone. You will need shoes."

She glanced at the string of smoked trout. I had the feeling that the Longknifes were planning to stay on with me through the winter.

Helen got up and went over to her pack, unfastened her snowshoes, and handed them to me.

"Put them on," she said. "See if they are right. If they are not right, my husband will fix them."

But the biggest gift of all followed the gift of the snowshoes.

"You need a door," Helen Longknife said. "Many animals in the forest will look for food when snow comes. They will walk right in on you when you are sleeping. The small animals, foxes and bobcats, they are not important. But we have wolves and bears. The bears are big. You need a door."

John Longknife took the planks I had bound together, which now stood aslant the opening, and laid them out on the ground. He cut hinges of a double thickness, using deerhide I had stored. With my jackknife and his hunting knife and a tool he had made and carried in his belt, on a key ring he had found somewhere that had two big rusty keys hanging from it, he bored holes and made wooden pegs. He wedged the frame I had made hard against the rock and set flat stones at the top and bottom and sides. He made an oak bar that moved on a heavy oak peg and locked itself into an oak slat.

I helped him as best I could. In four days the door was up. It fitted the frame, swung freely on its hinges, and could be barred tight from the inside.

When the door was finished, the Longknifes took their fish down, packed their things, and left.

"We would like to come next summer and fish," Helen Longknife said.

"You are welcome," I said.

"Then we will help you set the dugout in the water."

"Thank you."

The little girl came over and put her hand in mine for a moment.

I watched the family go down the slope. They had a birch canoe beached on the lake. As they moved away, they waved and I waved back. I liked them. They were friendly people. But for some reason I was not sorry to see them go.

It was mostly that I had grown comfortable in my new life. I had a warm cave for a home. A stream full of small fish and a lake teeming with large trout and wild fowl lay at my doorstep. The forest yielded an endless store of acorns and roots, nuts and berries.

And not only had I become comfortable, now I found myself looking forward to each day. I felt that I had a part in what it would bring. That each new day was not something that would just happen, but was something that I would make with my own hands and thoughts. I still feared Captain Cunningham. I often saw his round face with his little onion eyes staring at me. But the war and the terrors had begun to fade in my memory.

27

Snow fell early in December, as John Longknife had predicted, and lasted for three days. When it ended, there were drifts around the mouth of the cave higher than my waist. The stream still ran, but Long Pond was covered with a sheet of ice that grew deeper every night, until by the middle of December it was a foot thick.

By then I could walk out on the lake without falling through, wearing my new snowshoes. I chopped three holes in the ice and, with the hooks my friends had left me, short lengths of deer sinew, and venison bait, I set lines at each of them. The first day I caught six large trout, two bass, and a pickerel, all of which I buried in a snowbank.

I set the lines every morning, weighing them down with rocks, and went out toward evening to see what I had caught. After a week I had enough fish to keep me for a month.

The next-to-the-last day I fished the ice, I noticed tracks along the shore where the stream ran out of the lake between two low hills. When I first saw them I thought they were bear tracks, but they turned out to have been left by a man who took large steps and seemed to be in a hurry.

I did not follow the tracks that day, seeing no reason to, but the next morning I discovered fresh ones in the same place. I thought that whoever it was might be fishing at the south end of the lake, which lay out of sight around a bend.

It was a bright day, with the sun glinting on the trees. As I started back home, carrying my lines, a string of fish, and my musket, I saw a flash of light at the edge of the lake a few steps off to my right. I went over to see what it was, thinking that it might be something, a piece of metal, I might use.

To my surprise it was a trap that was shining new, and in it was a muskrat. It had been caught by its two front paws, One of them it had gnawed off, and it was trying to gnaw off the other. There was much blood on the snow.

The animal stopped chewing at itself and

bared its teeth at me. I worked my way around until I was behind it. Quickly, with a foot and a hand, I opened the trap. The muskrat took a feeble step and fell on its side.

It had a thick coat of glossy brown fur, but it was an ugly thing, with a pudgy face and whiskers and a funny smell. I had a notion to kill the animal with a blow on the head. Anyway, it was going to bleed to death. I decided not to kill it and walked on. Then I turned back. Somehow, lying there in the snow, alone and bedeviled, it reminded me of myself. Of how I had felt when I first came to Long Pond.

I took off my shawl to protect my hands and picked it up. The animal made a noise, a thin groan, opened its mouth, but didn't try to bite me. I carried it home and put it beside the fire, though I was sure it would die before nightfall.

The muskrat was still alive in the morning. I gave it water, which it didn't drink. Then some of the fish left over from my supper, which it didn't eat. I went back to the lake where the trap was. I hadn't noticed before that it had letters on it, scratched there by a chisel. The letters spelled the name Goshen. It gave me a start. Sam Goshen! Again I saw his long, purplish nose as he grasped me and shoved my body against the wagon wheel.

Farther along was another trap; this one was

unsprung. I sprung it. I found a second trap with a dead raccoon in it. I took the animal out. I found two more traps with dead beaver caught in them and ten more traps unsprung. I sprung them all and went home with the two beaver. I did not see Sam Goshen anywhere, but I was breathing hard when I got to the cave.

The muskrat was still alive. It would not eat or drink, but spent the evening licking the stump of its chewed-off paw. Once it got up as if it wanted to flee somewhere, then lay down and went to sleep.

It was uglier than I had thought at first. Its back legs were partly webbed, and it had a flat, thick tail shaped like a flour scoop. But if I could tame it somehow, it would be company. Gabriel, the bat, had gone to sleep when the big snow fell. He hung upside down now in a far corner of the cave, unconcerned about the new boarder or about me.

I barred myself in that night and cocked the musket and set it up handy. I half-expected Sam Goshen to come to the door. If he was around, he would surely see my tracks and follow them to the cave. If he did, I'd be ready.

I stayed up late, but he didn't come. Just before I went to bed I heard sounds outside. I crept over to the door, opened it a crack, and peered out. It was a bear snuffling around in the snow-bank where I had put the fish. He came and sniffed at the door for a while. Then I heard him trotting down the hill, breaking the dry crust along the trail.

28

In the morning I went down to the lake to set my lines. On the way I saw tracks along the stream where the bear had been fishing through the ice.

The tracks cut off across the lower part of the lake and disappeared into the brush. More likely he was now holed up for the winter. But while I was setting my lines I kept an eye out. For Sam Goshen, also, though I hoped that he had gone off somewhere else to put out a trap line and wouldn't be back for days.

The snowshoes made walking easier, but I was not used to them yet and while I was crossing the lower part of the lake on my way home, with the musket cocked on my shoulder, I stumbled and fell. No one had seen me fall, but I looked around and felt embarrassed.

As I sat there getting my breath, I heard a sound. It was behind me, along the edge of the lake where black sedges stuck up through the ice. It's the bear, I thought. He has come back and is trailing me.

I tightened the straps on my snowshoes and got up. I heard another sound. This time it wasn't the sound of an animal. It was human, a long-drawn-out moan that chilled me.

There was a clump of mountain laurel just beyond the sedges. The sounds seemed to come from that direction. I walked toward them, through the stiff grass and the dark laurel. On the far side, I stopped.

A man was sprawled out in the snow. He was raising his arms over his head and clenching his fists. His head was on one side. Where he was breathing, the snow had melted away and left a grassy place.

I thought that the man had shot himself somehow, but there wasn't any blood around. Then I saw that one of his legs was caught in a trap. It was a big trap, a bear trap, and it had him tight, right below the knee.

The man must have become aware that someone was standing there, for he stopped the moaning. He moved his head around and looked up.

His eyes were glassy; then they cleared a little. He opened his lips to say something but didn't speak. I couldn't mistake the eyes — I had seen them close — and the big purplish nose and the mouth stuffed full of yellow teeth. It was Sam Goshen, lying there with his leg in the bear trap.

There is no way now to tell how I felt. No way at all. I stared at him, holding my breath and staring. I took a step backward and leveled the musket. As I did so, a verse from Proverbs went through my mind. "He that passeth by, and meddleth with strife belonging not to him, is like one that taketh a dog by the ears." Certainly the strife did not belong to me. It belonged to Sam Goshen. It was none of my business if he had got himself caught in a bear trap. Before long he would die. And that would be the end of him.

I turned away. I walked along the edge of the lake, then stopped when he screamed again. I went back and stood over him. There was no sign that he recognized me. But he knew someone was standing there.

"Help," he said.

The word sounded like a frog croak.

I gathered up a handful of snow, pressed it together, and put it to his mouth. He wanted more, and I got it. Still, there was no sign that he knew who I was. He lay quiet for a while.

"Can you hear me?" I said.

He began to moan.

"Sit up," I said. "I'll help."

The trap was fastened to a heavy chain, and the end of it was wrapped around an elm tree. He had floundered about trying to get himself loose and made a half-circle where there wasn't much snow. I got him on his side so that the trap was between us.

"You pull," I said. "Then I'll pull."

Goshen took hold of one side. His hands were cut and bleeding from clawing at it. The blood was frozen in beads. I took hold of the other side of the trap. It had sawteeth that would have fitted neatly together with the other side if his leg hadn't been caught between them.

With my fingers between the iron teeth, I pulled, using all my strength. We both pulled, but I pulled harder than he did. Only the jaws on my side of the trap opened. Goshen's fingers turned white. His grip loosened. He fell back and lay still. I thought he was dead.

After a while he roused himself and sat up. He felt his leg where the jaws were biting into it. He had torn his legging away and I could see the rusty teeth half-buried in his flesh.

"It's not broken," he said, "but I feel my blood gettin' poison in it."

"How long have you been here?" I asked, as if we had met in the street and were talking.

148

"Two hours," he said. "Maybe more. Long enough to get poison."

I thought of asking him how he got himself caught, but didn't.

"Let's try again," he said and moaned.

This time, with him pulling harder, we got the jaws open far enough so that I could jam the butt of my musket between them and slide the trap off his leg.

Goshen let out a yell. He stood up, a freed man. He tried to take a step. He groaned and fell backward in the trampled snow and lay quiet.

He glanced up and said, "I know you. You're the one who got mad with me 'cause I said you were pretty. You camped around here? I've got to rest for a spell. My strength's run thin."

I said nothing and walked away. I crossed the lake and was starting up the stream when I heard the scream again. It made me remember that I had left my musket back there in the bear trap.

Goshen was on his knees, crawling toward me, when I got back. I pried my musket out of the trap. The pretty walnut stock had two deep scratches on it from the iron teeth. I got mad clear through, thinking that I had taken good care of the musket.

"Get out!" I shouted at him. "I don't want you here."

He was crouched on his knees looking up at

me. "I'm tryin'," he said, "but my leg won't work. It hurts somethin' terrible."

"You can get yourself to Ridgeford village."

"It's too far. Too far. I'd never make it with the snow and everything. I can feel the poison creepin' through my leg already."

He tried to get on his feet and fell. He was not putting on. I could tell that. It was very cold, but there was sweat on his face.

"You must have a tent somewhere," I said.

"I been travelin' light. I ain't got none. Just blankets."

"Where's your shaggy dog?" I asked, thinking that it might be sneaking up behind me, getting ready to bite.

"Back in the village," Goshen said. "Chewed up two prime pelts last time I had him out."

I don't know how I got him to his feet, except that he was a spare man, mostly bones. But somehow I got an arm around him and one of his around me, and we started off across the ice. We had to stop every few minutes to rest. Going up the hill we rested every two or three steps.

Sam Goshen was out of his head now. "I can feel the poison creepin'," he would say. Then he'd say, "It's got into my gizzards," or "The poison's got me, sure."

"What poison? You keep talking about it."

"Poison meat," he said. "Baited the trap with it."

Good enough for you, I thought.

A short piece from the cave he collapsed, and I had to drag him the rest of the way.

29

I built a fire in the far end of the cave, away from mine, put out snow water to heat. I didn't own a kettle, so I had to heat rocks and drop them into a big gourd I had cut in half. Then I laid out one of my mats by the fire and dragged Goshen across the cave and rolled him onto it.

He didn't say anything while I was doing this, though he kept on mumbling some sort of nonsense. I guessed that he must be out of his head with the pain.

I didn't know anything about fixing a leg that had been caught in a bear trap, but I washed out the places where the teeth had gone deep down. He came to before I finished, long enough to say:

"You got any bear grease? That's best for this sorta hurt."

"I have deer tallow."

"Not good as bear."

He spoke as if it were my fault, as if I should go out right away and shoot a bear and make him a pot of grease. I brought the deer tallow and let him put it on. By noon his leg had swollen up about twice the size it should be. By nightfall, however, he said he felt better and that he was hungry. "Had nary a morsel in more than two days' time."

I cooked him a trout and gave him some tea. He fell asleep while he was eating. I put the musket by my side with my hand on the barrel when I went to bed. But I was not afraid to sleep. Goshen's leg was hurting too much for him to bother me.

In the morning I heated water again and helped him soak his leg and use the last of the deer tallow, which I had planned to use to make candles. He slept most of the day, waking up once to crawl out into the bushes and once to ask me what there was for supper.

"I got a hankerin' for a cut of venison," he told me.

The day was cold, with a gray sky to the north and the feel of snow. I went out with my ax and chopped down a birch sapling. I sat by the fire and whittled out a crutch. Mr. Goshen eyed me from his corner, watching the jackknife cutting the soft, white wood.

"What you up to?" he asked me. "I don't remember your name."

"Making a crutch," I said, not giving him my name.

"You want to be shut of me, I can see plain enough."

"A crutch will give you something to get around on."

"I can't move nowhere, the shape I'm in. Crutch or no crutch." He sat up and explored his leg. "Maybe in a week I can get around a little."

The thought of being in the room with Sam Goshen for a week made a big knot in my stomach. His gun was lying down by the tree where he had got himself caught in the trap. I didn't know whether he had a knife or not. Mine I kept hidden. I felt funny about it, but I carried the musket around with me whatever I was doing. I was terrified, but tried hard not to be.

I cooked him a strip of venison for his supper. He ate all of it and asked for more, which I took to be a sign that he was getting better.

"My wife, Verna," he said, "she was my first wife, had a way of fixin' venison that you might like to hear about someday. It's vinegar that makes the difference. Not that yours warn't good, but bein' young and jest startin', it might hep you to catch a husband. Nothing like tasty vittles to soften a man's heart and innards. I know that for a fact, miss. I'm feelin' it now." He gave me a wink.

At dawn I went down to the lake and picked up Goshen's musket. It had a charge in it, which I poured out on the ground. I took his powder horn and did the same with it. I hid his musket in the grass.

It was snowing by then, feathery flakes, but by nightfall it was coming hard. In the morning, early, the snow turned icy. Goshen hobbled to the door and went out, using the crutch.

"Looks bad," he said when he came back. "Looks like it might sleet all day. Lucky we got fires burnin' and plenty of grub to fill ourselves."

I had put away food for the winter, planning everything carefully, and here I was, saddled with an extra mouth to feed. He had a big appetite now, sick as he was. What could it be when he got well?

"We don't have plenty of food," I said.

"You're forgettin', miss, that I'm a hunter." He lay beside my fire, not his, and raised his hands, as though to aim a gun, and made a clicking noise that sounded like a trigger going off. "I can shoot you a deer before you ever blink an eye."

Yes, a hunter, I thought scornfully, who gets himself caught in a bear trap. But I kept the thought to myself. I was deathly afraid of rousing his temper. I had seen none of it, but I was certain it was there, hiding behind the eyes that never looked straight at you, but around.

"You're a hunter," I said; "you must be acquainted with John Longknife."

Goshen thought for a moment, bending over. His hair grew in patches, and between the patches I could see the bones on top of his head. There were three ridges of them running front to back. In the firelight they didn't seem to fit each other.

"Longknife," he said. "Tall. Wears hair on his face?"

"No, he's an Indian," I said. "He was here last week with his family."

"Longknife," Goshen said. "Yes, I recall. No-good Indian. One of the Titicut tribe."

"He's coming back. He said today. I guess the storm held him up."

I tried to make the lie sound natural.

Goshen got on his feet and put the crutch under his arm and went back to his own fire. He asked for more wood. After I brought it, he said,

"Me and Longknife don't get along too good.

Claims I owe him for two beaver pelts he got off me in a trade. Claims I said they were prime and they warn't."

He said no more about John Longknife, but I could tell he was thinking. It would make him think hard if there was a chance that the Indian might come up the trail and find him causing trouble.

30

I fixed supper again for us, roasting two trout in the coals and making flour cakes. While we were eating there was a scratching, and the muskrat wandered out of the hole he had been living in since I brought him home. His chewed paw was pretty well healed, but he had a limp as he walked and a list to one side.

Goshen, who had not seen him before, stopped eating. "Hell and high water," he sputtered, "where did you find that?"

"In one of your traps," I said.

Firelight shone on the animal's glossy coat.

"Prime pelt," Goshen said. "It'll bring good money."

"It's not for sale," I said.

He didn't hear me. "Buy you a length of linsey-woolsey," he went on, "a ribbon for your hair, and a comb with sparklers in it."

The muskrat went back in its hole, frightened, I think, by the tone of his voice.

After supper I got out the Bible and started to read. He asked me if I would mind reading out loud.

"Haven't heard the Holy Book since I was at my dear ma's knee."

I had turned to Proverbs. I read while he leaned forward and cupped his ears.

" 'As snow in summer, and as rain in harvest, so honor is not seemly for a fool.' "

"Makes powerful sense," Sam Goshen said.

" 'A whip for the horse,' " I read, " 'a bridle for the ass, and a rod for the fool's back.' "

"Right smart talk," Goshen said. He looked around for the muskrat. "Fine pelt, that one. I'll catch me a few when my leg's aworkin'."

There was no sign that he understood what I was reading or why I was reading it. I decided to try another part of the Bible, the story of Jael. He waited impatiently for me to turn the pages.

" 'And the Lord discomfited Sisera,' " I read, speaking slowly, " 'and all his chariots.' "

"How many chariots?" Goshen broke in.

"Nine hundred, made of iron," I said.

"And who's this Sisera, anyway?"

"He was the captain of the armies of Jabin, King of Canaan."

"Go on, miss."

" 'The Lord discomfited Sisera,' " I said, " 'and all his chariots, and all his host, with the edge of the sword before Barak; so that Sisera lighted down off his chariot, and fled away on his feet . . .

" 'Howbeit Sisera fled away . . . to the tent of Jael the wife of Heber the Kenite . . . And Jael went out to meet Sisera, and said unto him, Turn in, my lord, turn in to me; fear not. And when he had turned in unto her in the tent, she covered him with a mantle.' "

"Why for?" Goshen asked.

"To protect him," I said, "or so Sisera thought."

"Some womenfolks are sly."

I read on. " 'And he said unto her. Give me, I pray thee, a little water to drink; for I am thirsty. And she opened a bottle of milk, and gave him drink, and covered him. Again he said to her, Stand in the door of the tent, and it shall be, when any man doth come and inquire of thee, and say, Is there any man here? that thou shalt say, No.' "

"I'm listenin'," Sam Goshen said.

" 'Then Jael Heber's wife took a nail of the tent, and took an hammer in her hand, and went softly unto him, and smote the nail into his temples, and fastened it into the ground for he was fast asleep and weary. So he died.' "

160

I stopped reading. Goshen waited with his mouth open. I closed the book.

"That all there's to it?" he said. "She kilt him?"

"Dead."

"With a nail?"

"With a long nail in his temple."

Sam Goshen stared across the fire at me with his cruel little eyes. He pawed at his own temple with two fingers. "A nail. That would hurt a man bad," he said. "No tellin' what some women-folks'll do if they get riled up."

"No telling," I said.

He started to laugh and then started on a rambling story about one of his wives who got mad and hit him on the head with a length of sycamore wood. But I think he knew why I had read him the story of Jael and Sisera. Whether it had done any good or not, I didn't know. It might have stirred him up to harm me.

He didn't see the white bat until days later, although it had been hanging there above his head all the time he was nursing his leg. He was eating a bowl of morning mush when he happened to glance up and see it. It made him jump. He forgot he had a bad leg. He scrambled to his feet and picked up his crutch.

"Bad luck!" he cried. "A white one, too. They're the worst."

He raised the crutch and took a swipe at the

161

creature. Before he could raise his hand again, I grabbed the crutch and threw it into the fire. I didn't say anything.

He pulled the crutch out and wiped it off on his sleeve. "I guess you think I don't need it no more. True enough; not much around the house here, but outside, that's different."

He put on his heavy coat and his flap-eared cap. He opened the door and glanced out.

" 'Pears to be a good day for huntin'," he said. "I think I'll go and shoot us a deer. You don't mind if I take your Brown Bess along?"

I held the musket in my hand. I never put it down anymore.

"You have a musket of your own," I said.

Mr. Goshen smiled, showing his mouthful of yellow teeth. "So I have, so I have," he said. "But I plumb forgot where I done left it. With my fever and all. It makes a man forgetful, fever does."

"Your musket is down on the shore," I said. "Where the bear trap is."

He put the crutch under his arm and tried his weight on it. He teetered back and forth and looked pained.

"Still hurts," he said. "But I'll bring you back a deer or die atryin'."

I opened the door and watched him hobble off.

It was a bright day, with the sun glistening on the snowbanks and blue drifts piled up along the lake. He was halfway down the slope when he disappeared behind a thick stand of mountain laurel.

After a while I caught a glimpse of him on the far side of the lake. He had dropped his crutch and was trotting along nimbly. Then he disappeared again.

I got hold of the muskrat and took it out in the sun and let it go. Or, rather, I gave it a push and made a noise I thought would urge it on. But it took a few steps, looked over its shoulder, and came back to the doorstep, where it sat the rest of the day in the sun until I took it in.

It was close to nightfall when I saw Sam Goshen coming up the hill. He had the crutch under his arm again and was picking his way slowly between the rocks.

I closed the door and set the bar. I waited for his knock. When it came, I didn't answer.

"I seen deer," Goshen shouted through the door. "Seven fat ones, trailin' along pretty as you please. But somebody done took my powder horn. Couldn't find my musket, neither. It might be that good-for-nothin' Longknife." He paused and I heard his heavy breathing. "'Course, it could be someone besides him."

I kept quiet.

"Now who'd ever do a thing like that?" he asked.

He sounded pitiful, but wasn't. He was mad. I could imagine his face through the thick wooden door, glaring and ugly. "Can't see who'd be so low-down mean." He cleared his throat and spat. "It wouldn't be you who done it, would it be, miss?"

"Yes, it was," I said. "And if you don't leave me alone, I'm going to do worse. A lot worse. I'm going to shoot clean through the door and maybe kill you."

There were no sounds for a while. I thought that he'd sat down to wait me out. Then I heard a lot of curses. Afterward, I heard footsteps going fast down the trail. I didn't look out. I stayed up all night, thinking he might come back. I heard every sound — wolves howling on the hill beyond, the lake cracking and booming, the wind in the winter trees, the cry of a bobcat, and, far away, a night owl calling.

But I heard no footsteps. Dawn came before I went to sleep.

I slept all that day, as closed to the world as Gabriel the bat. When I opened my eyes I lay and looked at the creature hanging upside down, wrapped in its silken wings. I closed my eyes, thinking that it would be nice if people, when things got bad, could wrap themselves up and go to sleep.

The fire was out when I woke up near midnight, and I had to build a new one, using powder, which I was short of. (At home, if the fire went out you could go to neighbors and borrow some coals.) But it was wonderful not to look over and see Sam Goshen lying in the corner. I hadn't realized how scared I had been all the time he was there.

I opened the door and looked out. A few stars glittered far down in the south. But northward the sky was black and a north wind blew hard.

31

I worked on the dugout that night. I had hollowed out a good part of the pine log by fire, and now I chipped away at the rest with the ax. It was beginning to take on the right shape, at least the shape I had in mind from what John Longknife had told me.

My reading of the Bible to Sam Goshen was only the second time I had opened the Holy Book since my father's death. I brought it out again and leafed through it, reading from whatever I happened to turn to. First it was Judges. Then Chronicles. Then Daniel and Hosea. Lastly, it was from the Book of Esther.

"And when these days were expired, the king

made a feast unto all the people . . . white, green, and blue, hangings, fastened with cords of fine linen and purple to silver rings and pillars of marble: the beds were of gold and silver, upon a pavement of red, and blue, and white, and black, marble."

When I was a child my father used to read this part of Esther's story to me. He was a frugal man, frugal because we were poor and by his own leanings, but he always liked these words and the scenes they pictured. I liked them, too. I would ask him to read again and again about Ahasuerus, the king, who reigned over a hundred and twenty-seven provinces, from India as far westward as the land of Ethiopia, who gave a grand feast for all his servants and nobles and the princes of Persia and Media in that marvelous palace of Shushan.

As I sat there by the fire, I read out loud to myself. The words made strange sounds among the stone walls of the cave and the soughing of the bitter wind, not the warm and exciting sounds I remembered as a child.

The north wind blew all night, and at dawn it began to snow and snow fell for five days, never stopping. When I opened the door, a wall of piled-up snow loomed before me, shoulder-high. I dug a path through it and away from the mouth of the cave. The earth was white as far as the eye could reach. Along the ridge above the cave the pine trees looked like white candles.

A herd of deer came to the edge of the path I had cleared. I think it was the same herd that I had driven away. Their eyes were half-closed with ice. They were cold and starving.

I went out and cut through the snow where it was thinner under the trees, down to within inches of the earth, close enough to the dry grass for the deer to feed. It took me three days, working half a day at a time. As I carted the snow aside and cleared a place, the deer came along grazing behind me.

The wind blew again, this time from the east. The smoke hole in the roof was covered with brush but the wind found its way in. It scattered ashes everywhere. The cave was freezing cold. I bundled up in the rush mat I used on the floor and huddled against the log fire. I sat and thought about the tavern in Ridgeford and how warm it would be in the kitchen and how good bread with real flour in it would taste.

The east wind lasted for two days. It ended in the night. The sun came up strong in a blue sky that glittered.

I had run out of tea and sweetening — Sam Goshen was responsible for this — and out of powder and shot, and I needed another blanket. I was in dire need of everything, but I didn't want to make the long journey to Ridgeford. Not because it would take all of three days coming and going in the heavy snow, but because I still lived in fear of the British. They had captured the town of White Plains a few days after I left the Golden Arrow, or so I had learned from Sam Goshen. By now they might have marched north and captured the whole countryside. The ferryman had said that they wouldn't bother to follow me, but I hadn't believed him. I didn't believe him now.

I worried over this for a day; then decided I must risk the chance, whatever happened. Wearing my snowshoes, I crossed the frozen lake at dawn and set off through the forest. The trail I had traveled before was hidden deep under the snow.

I came to Ridgeford at dusk of the second day. I circled the village, hiding in the trees, and looked for signs of the King's men. I saw nothing suspicious. The village looked the same as it had the day I left it, except that there were not as many carts on the street.

I went to the tavern, around to the kitchen door first, and talked to a boy who was coming out with a tray of food. I learned that there were no King's men inside, but many of their sympathizers were, now that they were winning the war.

I slipped through a side door into the ladies'
parlor. Just outside the parlor was the board
where they put up notices. A drover stood reading
a notice that looked to be new. I waited until he
turned away.

There were five notices on the board. Two
wanted to know the whereabouts of a deserter
from His Majesty's Ship *Rainbow*. Two concerned runaway slaves from a plantation in Vir-
ginia. One concerned a felon who had escaped
from Hartford Prison.

I read the notices twice. My name was not
there. I felt better. I felt almost calm. With my
last pence, I went down to the kitchen and made
a bargain with the cook to let me sleep that night
beside the oven. I still was uneasy about sleeping
upstairs in the tavern, even though my name was
not posted on the notice board.

32

When I showed Mrs. Thorpe, the cook, that I cold bake good bread, she took me on as a helper. Sometimes I had to carry trays into the tavern and set them on the serving table. I always hurried in and out and never looked at anyone or spoke.

I worked six days. With the shillings I earned I went across the street to Morton and Son's store. Young Mr. Morton waited on me. I thought he would recognize me, but he didn't seem to, and I acted as if I hadn't seen him peering at me over the pile of boxes the first time I had visited the store.

I bought gunpowder and shot, a jug of molasses, salt, and a package of tea. I would have bought more, but I lacked the money. When I asked for the tea, Mr. Morton set out three boxes.

"Just today we had a shipment from New York," he said. "It's the first in a long time. Now that the British are winning the war, we'll have tea regularly. What kind does thee wish? We have three brands, all from Ceylon."

I chose the least expensive and after he had wrapped it up and taken my money, he walked to the door with me. He held out his hand to say goodbye. It was pale, like his face. He had blue eyes and lanky, hay-colored hair, which he wore tied in a string knot. I still was sure that he hadn't recognized me.

"What is thy name?" he asked.

Sarah Bishop, I nearly blurted out. Then I caught myself in time and said, "Travers. Amy Travers." Amy was my cousin in Midhurst, England.

"Pretty name," he said. "Thee was in the store last year late. Thee bought an ax, powder and ball, flour, and salt. Thee wanted three or four blankets, but had money only for two."

"You have a good memory," I said. "But you forgot that I bought sweetening, too."

Mr. Morton smiled a little. Then he was serious again.

"Thee may think me rude," he said, "but I am not. There was a notice in the tavern. It was there before Christmas. It was signed by a Captain Cunningham and offered a reward for the return of a girl named Sarah Bishop, accused of starting a fire in New York City. It had a description of the girl. As I remember, it said she was tall yet slight of build and had blue eyes and freckles."

Mr. Morton looked at me as if he were certain that I was Sarah Bishop. As if all he need do was to march me down to the constable and collect Captain Cunningham's reward. I thought to flee out the door but he was standing against it.

"I don't know," he said, "whether thee is Sarah Bishop or not, though I am certain that if thee is not, then thee has a sister and her name is Sarah Bishop."

He smiled in a superior way at what he must have felt was a joke.

"But this is of little consequence," he said. "What I wish to say is that I remembered thee from the time thee first visited the store. And being most disturbed that thee was the Sarah Bishop responsible for the fire, I went to the tavern the next day after I saw the notice and took it down and destroyed it."

"Thank you," I managed to stammer. "That was kind."

He was looking at the musket I had under my arm.

"Why does thee carry that around with thee?" he said.

I knew well why I carried the musket, but I did not tell him.

He opened the door. Chill air rushed in, and he closed the door and stood with his back against it.

"My father waited on thee," young Mr. Morton said. "I heard thee tell him that thee wasn't settling around here, but going northward."

"Yes, something like that."

He was looking close at me, yet not unfriendly.

"I take it thee never went."

What business is it of yours? I had a mind to say, but I said nothing and edged toward the door. And how do you know that I didn't go north? I thought.

"Sam Goshen was in here a week ago to sell furs," Mr. Morton said. "He told us that there was a girl living up on Long Pond and described thee. I decided that thee must be the girl he was talking about."

It made me uneasy when he brought all this up. "I have a way to go," I said. "I'd better start."

Young Mr. Morton put out a hand to hold me back.

"My great-grandfather," he said, "was banished from Massachusetts Colony because he

174

broke the law by appearing in the street without a musket. But there's no law now that compels thee to carry one. What is thee afraid of?"

"Most things," I said, "and all people."

"Fear is something that encourages people to harm thee. Fear causes hatred."

"You sound like a Quaker," I said.

"I am a Quaker," he replied.

Mr. Morton was dressed in a plain dark brown jacket and plain trousers bound at the knee. He wore a black hat with a wide brim that turned up at the sides and had earflaps. He looked like a Quaker. My father had always disliked the Quakers, their "thees" and "thys," and somber clothes. He couldn't stand the silence of their prideful ways.

"Is that why you are not off to the war?" I asked him, thinking of Chad. "Because you are one?"

"For that reason," Mr. Morton said.

He opened the door. Out of a gray sky it was beginning to snow.

"Thee'd best not go now," he said. "We can put thee up here for the night. My mother can."

I gathered up my purchases.

"We have Meetings," he said. "I wish thee would visit when things are again quiet. We have them every fourth Sunday. Thee would be most welcome to come."

"Sometime," I said, although I had no thought of ever going to a Quaker Meeting. My father in his grave would open his eyes and look at me in dismay.

Mr. Morton glanced out at the falling snow, then closed the door and once more stood against it, as if to bar my way.

"On sober thought," he said, "I think it foolish of thee to depart in this storm, though the British are at hand. I can hide thee until the storm is over. I have hidden the persecuted before."

"Thank you kindly," I said, "but I must go."

Mr. Morton took off his black hat with the flat crown and the flaps that looked like the wings of a tired seagull. Then he put it on again at a straighter angle. That was another habit that my father disliked, the business of wearing a hat at all times, even indoors.

Suddenly he asked, "Does thee live alone?"

"Yes."

"It is not good for a young girl to live that way. Is it because the British hound thee?"

"Partly."

"Why else?"

"Because I like to."

Mr. Morton seemed puzzled. "Has thee no family?"

"None. They are dead."

"Thee is an orphan, then?"

Having answered his question, I said nothing.

He stared hard at the ceiling; perhaps he was staring at heaven.

"When the British leave," he said, "as leave they will, thee must come to Ridgeford. I shall find thee a proper place to live, and gainful employment. Thee cannot live alone in the wilderness. What if thee was to injure thyself? Or fall ill of some disease? Who would know? Who would help thee? Who would care for thee?"

"No one," I said. "I can make do."

I thanked Mr. Morton for his kindness and slipped past. After I had crossed the street I glanced back. He was still standing in the doorway, looking at me through the falling snow.

33

I went back to the tavern to stay until the snow
ended, but soon afterward five of the King's
dragoons rode into the courtyard and stabled
their horses. It had stopped snowing, and I saw
the men from the kitchen window. Mrs. Thorpe
wanted me to carry out food to them, but I stole
away while they were eating their breakfast.

On my way to Ridgeford I had made slash
marks with my knife on some of the trees I
passed, high enough on the trunks not to be hidden by fallen snow and close enough together so
that I would not stray off. I had no trouble find-
ing the marks on my journey home. But I was
nearly frozen when I got there. I used some of the

gunpowder to start a fire and sat beside it for hours, until I thawed out.

Months before, when I had heard the bear snuffling around outside, he was digging up the fish I had put in the snowbank. I found this out when I went to get one for my supper and all of them were gone.

I cut holes in the ice, set three lines and caught another batch of trout and bass. This time I smoked them the way the Longknifes had, over a hickory-wood fire and slowly. Some I saved for the muskrat, who liked fresh trout, though he would eat them when they were frozen. I didn't need to worry about Gabriel. He still clung upside down, never uttering a sound, happily asleep in his dark corner.

Spring came overnight, it seemed. The lake groaned and boomed and then the ice broke up into floes that mild winds moved around. The maples came first, the young leaves red in the sunlight, then the pink leaves of the oaks. Dogwood flowered everywhere, and along the stream there were big swatches of blueberry buds.

Blue herons fished the shallows and a torrent of brown hawks flowed down from the east, flying low over the lake and silently disappearing. Geese came out of the north in dozens of glistening wedges. Gabriel began his nightly wanderings.

The muskrat grew restless and wandered around the cave, making curious noises. But if I took him outside he would come limping back before long, looking hurt, as if I had wanted to get rid of him. At last I took him to the lake, waded out, and let him loose. He followed me ashore and back to the cave. I took him to the lake once more. This time he turned over on his back, gave me a sidelong glance, flapped his fat tail, and was gone. He left behind only the strong smell of musk and a string of silvery bubbles.

I had mixed feelings as he swam away. I knew better, but still I felt deserted. I saw him again a few days later, when I was out fishing on the shore. He came swimming along, only his head showing, with another muskrat trailing behind him. The pair cavorted around for a while and spoiled the fishing. Late in the spring I saw them again. This time they had two glossy young muskrats in tow.

Staunchly, Gabriel stayed by me. He went off on his nightly wanderings and came back promptly at dawn, hung upside down in his corner, and from time to time during the day gave out his timid squeals. Sometimes, before he flew off at dusk, I played the broom game with him. He was much more human than our neighbor the muskrat.

The Longknifes came early in June. Their

baby had died during the winter, but the little girl was healthy and had grown tall. They brought news that the British still held New York, which meant that Captain Cunningham was sitting behind his desk in the big, gray building.

We pushed the dugout down the grassy slope and slid it into the lake. To my surprise — and I think to the Longknifes' — it didn't swamp or turn turtle, but floated on an even keel. John Longknife had promised to help me make a birch canoe someday.

"It will be much lighter than the dugout," his wife said. "You can carry a birch canoe on your back. Then you can travel from lake to lake and stream to stream."

The dugout is all I'll need, I wanted to say, but didn't because it would seem impolite.

The Longknifes fished for five days, and I fished with them. We smoked our trout together, enough to last well into the coming winter, which we were thinking about already. We hunted together — geese for tallow, using reed traps to save powder, and deer meat to smoke.

One evening when we came in from the lake we found tracks beside the stream, where the bear had been fishing. It was the same animal that had stolen my cache of fish from the snow-bank, judging from the way one of his front paws slanted out. I didn't mind the fish so much as I feared happening upon him sometime when I was alone.

"Should we track him down?" I said bravely, braver than I felt.

John Longknife shook his head. "One bullet no good. Two bullets no good. Three bullets maybe good." He turned to his wife and spoke in their language.

"My husband says," she explained, "that the bear moves quick. And you can kill him only in a certain place. If you miss that place you will not have time to load your musket again. He will jump on you and claw you dead."

At that moment I gave up the idea of shooting the bear with the paw that slanted out, the bear that stole my fish.

The Indians stayed for most of a week. Helen showed me how to brew tea from black birch leaves and bark. She also pointed out a hollow tree, on the ridge near the big rock that looked like a castle, where there were two swarms of of bees. In another month I could rob their hives, she told me. "But don't take all the honey. Take only half. The bees need the rest to eat during the winter."

Since they were on their way to Ridgeford to purchase supplies, I asked the Longknifes if they would take along a packet of deer meat and give it to young Mr. Morton. Whenever I thought of him, I felt sorry that he looked so thin and gaunt. As if he needed a good meal, one like I used to cook at home when we were all together.

The Longknifes glanced at each other and smiled when I mentioned his name, which embarrassed me. I explained that I had barely met Mr. Morton and felt sorry for him because he was so sickly-looking.

"His father owns a store where you can buy all sorts of food," I explained, "and yet he always looks hungry, as if he never ate a mouthful."

"He eats," Helen Longknife said, "but he has a fire inside."

"In trouble much," John Longknife added, "this man."

"They had him in the jail," Helen said. "It was because of the war. He would not go and they put him in jail. Then he got in arguments with his father. His father owns two Negro slave women and won't give them up. They got to fighting because he wouldn't, and Isaac Morton was put in the jail again."

"In jail much, this man," her husband said. "All the time jail."

I was not astounded to learn that Isaac Morton was in jail much of his time. Nor that he had a fire inside him, as Helen Longknife said. I saw all of it in his eyes when he was talking to me, smoldering there quietly.

Helen asked, "Shall I say something to Mr. Morton? Do you want to send some words?"

"Nothing," I said. Then I changed my mind. "Tell him he's too skinny. He needs to eat more."

Helen was disappointed. "Is that all you are saying?"

Even that is too much, I thought. Why should I bother with whether he was skinny or not? Why should I be giving him advice?

"Don't say anything," I said. "Just give Mr. Morton the venison. He should know what to do with it."

The Longknifes left in a thunderstorm, weighed down with pelts they had taken that winter. They planned to drop by on their way home, so they cached the fish they had smoked.

When they got to the far side of the lake and stood on the big rock, they stopped and waved. I had a tight feeling in my throat as I waved back. I was surprised that I was sorry to see them go.

34

Two days after they left I took a notion to explore the big rock where I had last seen the Longknifes, the rock that looked like the battlements of an English castle. Early in the morning I paddled the dugout to the base of the towering walls, beached it, and climbed through heavy brush to the top.

Far below me the lake shimmered in the morning sun. The water was many shades of blue, but black deep down. I felt as if I were on a castle wall in England, on a battlement looking down into a darksome mere. I saw a shadow there below in the deep water. It was mine. It was beckoning to me.

I took a small step forward and grasped hold

of an arching branch to steady myself. At that instant I felt a sharp sting on my hand. I drew back. I though it was the sting of a hornet, of which there were multitudes. But then I saw a pair of yellow eyes staring down from a ledge. The eyes were dark with yellow slits, bulging out of a flattened head. A black tongue flicked at me. I caught a glimpse of banded coils, brown and ruddy-brown. It was a copperhead.

I had seen these snakes before on the farm early in May when they first came out from their winter sleep. I had watched while two of these copperheads — Father said they were males — went through a dance. They rose as high as they could and pushed against each other, until one of them fell over.

I knew that the copperhead was a poisonous snake . . . because one of our neighbors was bitten and died from the bite.

My hand had two holes in it. It felt numb as I scrambled down the cliff and into the dugout, but it didn't hurt. I had no trouble using the paddle, and I thought maybe the snake wasn't a copperhead after all. Then my hand began to swell and my lips started to tingle. Then I got sick to my stomach.

I went up the slope to the cave and lay there in the doorway. My left hand was now twice the size of the other one. The two holes were puffed up and blue-colored. Remembering what my father had once told me, I got out his knife and made two cross-slits where the bite was and sucked the blood away.

My whole hand was swelling now. It was blue and black, with long streaks of yellow running up my arm. I shouted with all my breath, but no one answered. A flight of geese circled the lake, calling to each other. A crested jay silently watched me from a pine tree. I shouted again. There was not an answering sound from anywhere.

I got to my feet. My only thought now was to find my way to Ridgeford village somehow. I went down the hill to the lake and crawled into the dugout. I picked up the light, birch paddle. It was heavy as iron. It fell overboard and began to drift. I reached for it, but it kept moving away. It was like a feather floating away in the air.

Suddenly the sun went behind a cloud, or seemed to.

When I saw it again I was lying in the bottom of the dugout. It had floated across the lake into the sedges. How much time had gone, I do not know. A day? Two days? I have no memory how long I lay there.

The paddle was beside me. I don't remember ever taking it out of the water. My hand was the same size as my arm, but I looked at it and thought, I am not dead. I may die, but I am still alive.

I got to my knees and cupped water from the lake and drank it. It made me sick. Yet I felt stronger. I had strength enough to paddle the dugout through the sedges to the upper part of the lake. There I beached it and lay down on the shore and slept until the moon came up.

By its light I found my way to the cave. The fire had gone out, but there were two strips of venison left over from my last meal, whenever that was. I ate them and fell asleep again and slept until morning. I woke up thirsty. It took me a long time to get down to the lake.

I climbed into the dugout and slept again. I was awakened by a flock of geese beating their wings and honking as if someone had disturbed them. I thought it might be the Longknifes returning. I waited all morning, but they did not come.

This was the first day I had felt strong enough even to think of making the long journey to Ridgeford. But I didn't move. I was afraid of the British. The reward for my capture might have been posted on the notice board again. I was more afraid of the British than of the copperhead bite, so I lay quiet in the sun.

A kingfisher swooped down and snatched a minnow from the lake and flew away with it crosswise in its beak. Small white clouds floated above me. I felt that I was high up in the sky and that they were white clouds floating on a blue sea. A muskrat swam close and glanced up, trailing beads of bright water from his muzzle. He could have been my friend with the three paws. He'd never had a name, so I tried to think of one now, but I couldn't. I watched the evening shadows fall. I felt lonely and afraid of the coming night.

I went back to the cave and built a fire and made tea and ate a small part of a smoked fish. I sat in the doorway for a while, watching the moon rise. A snowy owl swooped past. Wolves howled close by on the moonlit ridge.

That night I had a bad dream. At least, it must have been a dream, or else I would not have been alive in the morning. I was walking along the stream on my way to the lake just before dusk. I saw a shadow against a rock and heard a snuffling sound and heavy steps coming slowly toward me.

Whatever it was, it sounded much bigger than a wolf. I turned around. Not a dozen steps away was a black shape. An animal. Its head was down, as if it was sniffing at my footsteps. Then it raised up, and I saw that it was a black bear. It stood on its hind legs, swinging its head back and forth. Its mouth was open and its tongue lolled out.

The musket was primed. I pulled the trigger.

The shot came out of the muzzle slow and crooked. I loaded the musket again, but before I could bring it to my shoulder, the beast was upon me. Its red maw gaped open. Its teeth glistened for a moment, then the jaws snapped shut with a crunching sound, tight upon my head. I awakened weak and feverish.

The sun lay on the eastern ridge, but the fire had gone out and it was still night in the cave. I sat up. I felt my hand, which was still sore and stiff. I made a vow. When I got strong enough, I would climb the high rock and find the snake that had bitten me. I had meant it no harm. I was attending to my own business. I would lie in wait and kill it when it came out of its lair.

35

The Longknifes came back and found me stretched out in the cave beside a bed of cold ashes. Helen fed me dried venison and tea, which gave me strength, and made punk-wood poultices for my arm. In three days I was much better. At the end of a week I was on my feet once more.

We went down to the lake to fish. We were all in the dugout and ready to throw out our lines when Helen said she had a message for me from young Mr. Morton.

"He wants you to come to a Meeting. It's seven days from now."

"Have you been?" I asked.

"Two times."

"Good," John said. "Sit much. Say nothing. Eat much. Good."

"Quakers are kind people," Helen said. "They like Indians."

"Like much," John said. "Indians like 'em Quakers, too."

"There is much trouble in Ridgeford village," Helen said. "No rain for five weeks now. Corn has withered. Everyone worries about food for winter."

"It's been dry here at Waccabuc also. Some of the young birch and oaks are dying. But here it doesn't matter, because I am not growing anything."

"There is much sickness also in the village. They call it the flux."

"The war," I said. "What is happening?" I had tried to forget the British. I had tried hard, but I still dreamed at night about the gray hulk at Wallabout and David Whitlock leaning down to tell me in a croaking whisper that my brother was dead. I still heard the tearing sound of the shot the Hessian had fired at me. And at times during the day I saw our home aflame and our barn burning and the monstrous figure of my father staggering toward me through the smoke. "What is happening in the war, Helen?"

"The British came last month. They stood at one end of the village and fired cannons. No one fired back at them, so they marched away and didn't come back. But the drouth is bad and the sickness. People say that they are caused by a witch. Do you believe this could be true, that trouble can be caused by a witch?"

"It is silly, but sometimes I wonder."

"Myself, I believe in the witches." Helen was baiting a hook. She threw the hook into the water and gave me a worried glance. "Do you plan for the Meeting seven days from now?"

"I haven't planned."

"Mr. Morton wants you to."

"Perhaps."

"I hope you do."

I gave no more thought to the invitation until days later. Watching as the Longknifes packed their fish and left, I was overcome by a spell of loneliness. I thought about the British. I saw Captain Cunningham staring at me with his red-rimmed eyes. I heard the musket shot again. But I decided to go to the Meeting whatever happened.

The next morning I climbed the high battlement where the copperhead lived. I moved silently, as John Longknife had taught me to do. The snake's lair was a crevice beneath the exposed root of a tree. The sun shone into it. The copperhead was nowhere in sight. I hid myself behind a rock and waited, the musket cocked.

In midmorning, when the snake hadn't appeared, I returned to the cave and packed my things and left for Ridgeford village. There would be plenty of time after I got back to kill the copperhead.

I slept in the open that night, there being a warm wind blowing, and made a start as the cocks began to crow. I skirted the village as I had done before, thinking that the British might have returned since the Longknifes left. Likewise, I scouted around the stables. I noticed that beyond the tavern the fields were withered. I wondered about witches.

Mrs. Thorpe gave me breakfast for helping her with the bread. I cleaned myself up and combed my hair, which was a decent length by now.

I crossed the street to the Morton store and knocked. A Black girl came to the door. I told her that I wished to see young Mr. Morton. She must have been expecting me, for she let me in and led the way through the store to a parlor in the back. She pointed to a chair and asked me please to sit down.

I sat for a while with my hands in my lap. I felt uncomfortable in my threadbare dress. It was strange, sitting in a chair, with a rug on the floor and a clock ticking away and a glass window to look from. The window was open. I heard faint voices from somewhere beyond the parlor. I recognized young Mr. Morton's voice; afterward, his father's voice. They were arguing about something. Then there was a long silence.

Suddenly I heard my name, That is all I could make out, just "Sarah Bishop." It was the father who was speaking. I heard my name once more. This time it was shouted. Again it was the father speaking.

I had a strong temptation to get up and leave, for it was clear that they were talking about me. I did get up and was standing at the window when Isaac Morton came in. He was in sober clothes with his black hat on straight. He was smiling. It was a small, pinched smile, however, and his face was flushed.

"I hoped thee would come," he said.

He sat me down on a big sofa and then seated himself beside me, gingerly, on the edge.

"I didn't expect to," I said, just to let him know that I had not pined to come. "It is a long way to Ridgeford village."

"I prayed that thee would," he said. "And that the Lord would lighten thy footsteps."

I had a mind to tell Isaac Morton that the Lord had failed him. That I was still tired from the long walk and sleeping out on the hard ground and being in fear of the British.

"Would thee like some breakfast?" he asked.

"I have eaten, thank you."

"Then we should go," he said. "We are late, and the Meeting is two miles away."

I expected that he must have a carriage waiting outside or horses we could ride, but there was neither. The cart the Mortons owned held three people. In it were his mother and father and one of the Negro servants.

We walked down the street and turned off into a dusty road. The sun was hot. We walked for most of an hour. Mr. Morton took long, loping strides, but I managed to keep up with him. For the first mile he had nothing to say except that walking was good for the spirit.

We were walking along a winding road, between trees that met over our heads. The air was still and sprinkled with dust from the family carriage clopping along ahead of us.

"I have spoken to thee before about the musket," he said. "About carrying it around all the time. Here it is again, sitting atop thy shoulder on a Sunday morning. It looks peculiar, this being a peaceful community."

"Your father was curious about the musket," I said. "When I first came to Ridgeford, before I left, he asked about it." I was pretty certain that the argument I had overheard that morning was about me and the musket. "Your father doesn't like it, does he?"

Mr. Morton was silent. He looked up at the trees. He started to whistle a tune.

"He doesn't like me, either," I said.

"He read about thee on the notice board, Sarah."

This was the first time that Mr. Morton had called me by my first name. I liked hearing it. I wasn't worried much about what his father thought, not right then.

"We do not own a musket," he said.

"You live on a busy street, not out in the wilderness."

"We Quakers don't carry muskets."

"I am not a Quaker, I wish you to know."

"I do know it," Mr. Morton said, speaking low and, for him, quite sweetly. "I know it well. That is why I have invited thee to the Meeting."

My shoes were caked with dust. The sun was hot, despite the trees. I began to wonder why I had come.

"They will be talking about witchcraft at the Meeting," he said. "My father will. He believes in witches. Not the ones who ride about on broomsticks, but the others who live quietly among us and never raise their voices. I believed in witches until I was old enough to know better. Did thee?"

"Yes," I said. I didn't tell him that sometimes even now I wondered about them.

36

The Meeting took place at a farmhouse that belonged to a man named Peake. The house was large, and behind it were a number of barns and beyond them vast acres of corn. The corn looked sickly.

Carts and horses stood to one side in an oak grove. The Quakers were gathered by the house. Young Mr. Morton glanced at the musket and hesitated. Then he took my arm and started to lead me through the crowd, but I slipped away from him and found a place in the back.

He went up the steps and stood on the porch. Someone rang a bell, a small bell that scarcely made a sound. I was used to Sabbath bells that stirred you up inside. Mr. Morton held up his hands. It was a sign, I thought, for everyone to sing, as they always did the first thing in any church I had ever gone to. But there was only a big silence. People bowed their heads and prayed. I was the only one who didn't.

After the prayer ended, everyone stood around in silence, thinking his own thoughts, talking to himself, I guess, for it was very quiet.

Isaac Morton's father was standing not far away, close enough for me to see him crane his neck every once in a while. He didn't look at the musket because I held it behind me. He looked at me. He had eyes that stuck out of his head, like a frog's. They were cold, too, like a frog's eyes. I moved away where he couldn't see me.

After the long silence, he slid through the crowd and climbed up on the porch and stood beside his son. They talked for a few minutes; then he turned to the gathering and asked for their attention.

He had a croaking voice, like the frogs on Long Pond. It boomed out over the crowd, quieting them, even the children who were fidgeting. He spoke about the drouth and how it had lasted since the first days of August.

"Crops have withered in the fields," he said.

"Grapes upon the vine. The sun has risen, and the sun has gone down, each day in cloudless skies."

He paused and gazed above him at the wide blue sky. People followed his gaze. The sun poured down upon us. There was not a cloud in sight.

"Calamity," he said, "has come upon us while we were deep sunk in selfish thoughts. Heedless of God's words, as we were, it has visited us while we slept."

He stopped to drink from a cup his son handed him.

"The day has come for repentance," he said, speaking slowly in his booming voice. "And I, Thomas Morton, will be the first to repent, sinner that I am. Henceforth, from this day forward and forever, my two Negro slaves, Sue Curry and Amy Byrd, shall be free. From this moment on they may do as God wills them, without let or hindrance."

He paused, and his gaze traveled aimlessly over the crowd.

"If there are any," he said, "who like me have held slaves, who do own them now, I call upon you to follow my example."

A hush fell over the gathering. Two men moved out and went up on the porch and spoke a few words, freeing their slaves. He waited for others. When no one else came forward, he held up his hands and thanked God for the souls that had been freed.

Then he said, "We have seventy-three Friends here this morning. If not for the sickness that prevails, we would have twice that number. But many are frightened. Many are ill. Many are attending those who are ill. Some, alas, are dead."

A woman cried out in a grieving voice.

"Yet, dear people," Mr. Morton said, "the burdens of drouth and sickness that have been placed heavily upon our shoulders are not God's will alone. There is some evil presence among us in this village of Ridgeford, a malevolent spirit, call it what you will, that threatens our fortunes and our very lives."

Thomas Morton stood on the porch gazing down at us. The hot sun glinted on his sweating face. His gaze shifted back and forth, as if the evil presence he spoke about were somewhere near at hand, within the sound of his voice.

He never looked in my direction once. And yet I had the feeling that these threatening words were meant for me. He went on about the drouth and the sickness. The people grew restless. There were moans and painful words. I put the musket under my arm. Quietly, I made my way out of the crowd.

I reached the road that led to the village. A wind had sprung up, and on it I could hear Mr. Morton's booming voice. I thought I heard him speak my name.

I began to run. I heard footsteps. A hand reached out and grasped my arm.

37

At first, I thought it was Isaac Morton who held me. He had seen me leave and start down the road. I was ready to pull myself loose, without ever turning around.

"A moment, Sarah Bishop," a voice said. "I would have a word."

The man wore a red coat with two rows of brass buttons down the front. He is an officer, a British officer who has come to arrest me, I thought.

I glanced about in terror. There was heavy underbrush on both sides of the road and a thick stand of trees beyond. If I only could get loose, I would disappear into the trees and run. I wouldn't stop running until I reached home and barred the door behind me.

The man wore a brass badge with a single word stamped across it The word started with a "C"; the rest was blurred.

He said, "I am Constable Hawkins. I wish to detain you for a short while. Be calm."

A two-horse wagon drove up and stopped. In it was a youth with a nose peeling from the sun. The constable hustled me into the wagon and climbed up beside me. We drove to the far side of the village, across a stream that was mostly dry, to a run-down building standing among tall weeds. Here, Constable Hawkins took me by the arm and led me through a battered doorway.

"Our jail burned down last week," he apologized. "We have to use the old mill until we build a new one. Who knows when that will be?" He pointed to a bench. "Please seat yourself yonder."

"Why?" I shouted. "Why am I here?"

"You're here for protection," the constable said. He spoke gently, as if I were a child. "Be calm. I'll be coming back shortly, once the Meeting's over. When the people settle down. Right now they're pretty riled up about one thing and another. People dying and the two-headed calf that Coleman's heifer had. And the blue dog that was whelped over on the Thompson farm just yesterday noon. Not to mention the jail burning down. And it was a beauty if ever I saw one."

He backed out the door and closed it. I heard him fumbling with a key.

"You are locking the door!" I cried. "Why?"

"I've told you already. For protection. People are in a bad mood."

He rattled the door. I heard him walk away and the wagon start off at a clip. Was it possible that there were people in the village of Ridgeford who honestly thought I was a witch?

A bedraggled girl, a year or two older than I, sat astride the far end of the bench. She was knitting when I came in. She had stopped and now examined me through strands of tangled hair.

"I don't believe in witches and all that foolishness," she said. "Do you?"

I sat down on the bench and tried to answer, but my teeth were clenched with fright.

"A chancy world," someone crouching in the shadows said.

I hadn't seen her before and didn't see much of her now, except that she was a crone, stooped and old.

The mill was small. A set of worn grinding stones lay on their sides. There was a window high up. Through it I saw arching trees and white clouds. The constable had told me twice to be calm. I tried to be.

"I didn't know that witches were flying around nowadays. Thought they were all burned up long ago," the old woman murmured.

"Not all," the bedraggled girl said. "You look like a witch yourself."

The crone thought about this for a while, clucked to herself, and went on. "Grandmother was a witch. That was north of here, in Dedham, near Boston. They took her clothes off and beat her with a whip that had five braided tails. They beat her bloody. Drove her out of Boston city, as far as Dedham. She's buried there somewhere, my grandmother, without a stone to mark her."

I sat frozen to the bench. The two went on talking. After a while the crone fell asleep and the girl again took up her knitting. A woodpecker was hammering away at the side of the mill. He finally drilled a hole in the wood and a beam of light came through. The pecking stopped. Then the bird flew back and put an acorn into the hole, thinking to store it there, I guess, but it fell through and lit at my feet.

I sat quietly on the bench and tried to get my thoughts together. I had believed that Isaac Morton had asked me to the Meeting because he felt that I was godless and needed to be converted. I was wrong. He had invited me here to cause trouble. To have me run out of Ridgeford, out of the country.

I got to my feet and began to pace up and down. I carried the musket cocked on my shoulder. If Constable Hawkins had come back then, I think I would have put a ball in his carcass.

The girl said, "You make me nervous, walking around with that musket on your shoulder."

The crone laughed, a stringy laugh, and said, "Pretty quick, ducky darling, you'll be mounting that gun and be flying away like a true witch."

I aimed the musket over my head and pulled the trigger. The sound shook the building. Smoke billowed. Now there was a hole in the roof. The two left me alone.

I sat and thought about Long Pond. The mallards and brown-breasted pintails and ruddies, feeding in the marshes. The browsing deer and the sly fox that came for food every morning at dawn. The acorns that needed to be gathered and the blueberries that should be picked before the jaybirds got to them.

The woodpecker went on storing acorns that fell through on the floor. After a while I heard a horseman on the road. Then a wagon drew up. Then Constable Hawkins unlocked the door. Behind him stood Isaac Morton, his hat askew, as if he had ridden hard.

38

Constable Hawkins smiled. "I told you to calm yourself, that I'd be coming back," he said. "I needn't have brought you here in the first place, but I was scared the crowd would get at you."

Isaac Morton said. "I feared for thee, Sarah. I still do. Not for thy life now, not for that, but for other things. I'll tell thee."

He led me to his horse, which had been ridden fast and was unsaddled. "I borrowed her," he said. He made a step with his hands, gave me a boost, and I swung up in front. "She belongs to Jason Sharp. Someday I'll take her back. That is, if Jason pays the bill he's been owing for two years next month."

I had ridden sidesaddle on the farm, but not astride while my dress hiked up and my legs stuck out both sides. We went straight down the street, with people staring. We stopped at the tavern, and Isaac tied up the mare to the hitching post.

Mr. Cavendish, the tavernkeeper, walked past. It surprised me when he nodded to us in a pleasant way.

"He's with us," Isaac said. "It was Mr. Cavendish who settled the hotheads this morning. When they took to shouting and carrying on, he rose up and shamed them quiet. That was when thee was sitting there in jail, Sarah."

A cloud hid the sun but passed on, leaving the sky hot and brassy-looking.

"I am loath to say that my father, unlike Mr. Cavendish, does not like thee," Isaac said. "He has not liked thee from the beginning. Since the time when thee first came to the store. Thy hair was short, unwomanly. He did not admire that. Thee had a wild look in thy eyes, as if thee had seen a ghost. And that made him suspicious. Then there was the musket and thee saying, 'It's none of your business,' or something like that."

"I could have said this to your father because it wasn't any of his business. And it isn't now."

"Another thing. I have already mentioned it. He knew about the paper the British tacked up on the notice board. That struck him hard, since he is a staunch King's man. But there is more than the way thee looks and the musket and the way thee talks and the paper on the notice board. The Indian who was by thy place and claimed he owned it came into the store and told my father that thee had run him off. What's more, the Indian reported that thee had a bat up there in the cave and thee treated it like a person. Thee even talked to it."

"I did talk to it."

Isaac looked puzzle. "Anyway, the bat got Father to thinking even more. Then this morning when thee came, he started in on me. He said that I should not have invited thee to the Meeting."

"I am sorry you did invite me. And that I ever went to the Meeting."

"I am not. I am glad thee came. But we are in trouble."

"Not you."

"The two of us."

"I'll leave now and go back to Waccabuc. You'll not be responsible for me."

"They will reach thee, Sarah. Witch-hunting disappeared years ago, almost everywhere except in Ridgeford. Here they still believe in them. Whenever something bad happens, like drouth or a plague of crickets, they blame it on a witch. And they search until they find one."

"Who are these searchers?"

"My father is one," Isaac said. "He and the rest will search until they find someone they think is a witch. It happened six years ago. That spring we were burdened with a drouth and crickets; not so bad as this one, but bad. They snooped around day and night until they located an old woman — her name was Melanie Medwick. She looked like a witch, owned seven cats, four of them black, and lived alone in the abandoned mill you were in today. They tied her to the tail of a cart and whipped her out of Ridgeford. As a matter of fact, the drouth ended when they got rid of Melanie Medwick. That made them believe in witches all the more."

"These men are not the whole village," I said.

"But they rule it, Sarah. And they will try to hound thee as they did Melanie Medwick. Most likely they'll meet tomorrow. It's like a trial, though it isn't legal. They'll call witnesses. They'll pass sentence. If it goes against thee, then they'll try to run thee off Long Pond and keep thee from ever setting foot in the village."

"They can't run me off."

"Not legally. But they'll get at thee somehow. Thee will not be able to buy salt or flour or powder for thy musket in Ridgeford. If thee was living in a house, they would come in the night and burn it. Many people will not speak to thee on the street. Some of the children will throw rocks at

211

thee. They will find ways, surely enough, to get rid of thee."

"I'll not leave Long Pond."

"They are mean people, Sarah."

"I'll never leave," I said. "Should I speak out tomorrow?"

"Yes," Isaac said. "We shall both speak out."

After he left I went to the kitchen. For helping her with supper, Mrs. Thorpe gave me a place to stay. I never thought once that night of leaving Ridgeford, not before I had stood up and faced these men.

39

The Meeting began just past noon in the tavern, in a room upstairs where people played billiards. It was a big room with the billiard table in the center and chairs around two of the sides. There were many windows, some of them looked out upon the street and others upon a grove of elm trees and cornfields that stretched beyond.

The sun was beating down through a pearly haze on the dusty street when Isaac left the store and we met in front of the tavern. I thought it was a bad idea for us to meet together, boldly that way, but Isaac said not to mind.

They knew we were coming, because he had told his father. They were at the windows, looking down, when we climbed the steps.

Isaac took a Bible from his pocket. "I am going to read from Matthew," he said. "They have forgotten Matthew. And about thee, my advice is, be patient, speak softly, and tell the truth as thee knows it. Also, thee might do well to leave the musket in the hallway as thee goes in."

There were six of them sitting in a stiff row against the far wall, with all the windows open and the hot wind billowing the curtains back and forth. Off in the corner I saw Constable Hawkins and two men. One was the Indian who had come to Long Pond, the one I had run off. The other man was Sam Goshen.

Mr. Morton rose and said a short prayer. When he got through he glanced at me, then at the musket I still held in my hand. I was standing beside his son in the doorway. He said something to the other five men and they all stared at the musket. Then he motioned us into the room.

"Sarah Bishop," he said at once, "it is unusual for us to listen to words of the accused, but thee is of a tender age, and we wish to be fair and hear thee out."

"Thank you," I said, trying hard to swallow my anger.

"Thee is charged," he began, "with witchery of an evil nature. Said witchery has brought upon the God-fearing village of Ridgeford drouth that had laid waste our fields. It has brought into our midst a sickness, rampant sorrow, pain, and death." He paused to glance at his watch. "Does thee deny these charges?"

"Yes," I said. "I do deny them wholly."

"Proceed."

"I am not a witch. I live alone and mind my own business."

"Thee lives in a cave somewhere near?"

"On Long Pond."

"Why does thee live in a cave?" he asked in his raspy voice.

"Because it is comfortable."

"Why does thee not live in Ridgeford, like other God-fearing people?"

"Because I like Long Pond better."

"Why does thee choose to live alone?"

Memories flooded in upon me. I couldn't speak. The room was silent. A hot wind came through the east windows. Far off I could see clouds that were fleecy above and purple below. Isaac looked at me, hoping that I would answer, but I couldn't.

"Is that all thee wishes to say?" Mr. Morton asked.

I nodded. Words would not come.

He turned to the two men seated in the far corner. "Sam Goshen, will thee please step forward."

Goshen rose and with a limping gait took up a position in front of Mr. Morton.

"Goshen, did thee for a matter of five or six weeks spend time in the cave owned, at least lived in, by Sarah Bishop, who stands there?"

Sam Goshen touched his forelock and bowed. "Yes, sir, I remember I did live in the aforementioned cave, the one on Long Pond."

"What did thee observe while there? Anything out of the usual?"

"Everything was strangelike, sir."

"Be explicit, please."

"Well, one thing, she always had that musket to her shoulder. Except when she was asleep, and then she had it tucked away under herself and her hand tight on a half-cocked trigger."

Goshen took time to think.

"Go on," Mr. Morton said.

"For another thing, she had a muskrat running around. It only had three paws and was no good for nothin' except maybe a pelt."

"Did the animal act peculiar?"

"They all act peculiar, muskrats. There was one I caught last spring . . ."

Mr. Morton suggested that he reply to the question.

"She talked to it."

"What did she say?"

"I don't remember exact, but things you say to people."

"She talked to it as if it were a person?"

"Yes, and the muskrat answered back. Not words, mind you, but squeaks. It made my scalp tingle to hear them talkin'."

"What else, Mr. Goshen, did thee observe while living in the cave on Long Pond that would lead thee to believe that Sarah Bishop is a witch?"

"The bat, mostly. A white bat."

"A white bat?"

"Yes, white as driven snow."

"White is an odd color for a bat, is it not?"

"Never saw one afore in my whole life. And I'm forty-two and have run onto lots in my time. Black and brown sometimes, but nary a white one. Hope I never see one again."

"Did Sarah Bishop talk to the bat as she talked to the muskrat?"

"Sure."

"What else concerns the white bat?"

"She let it out as soon as the sun set and took it back in at crack of day."

"Where does thee think the bat went when she let it out?"

"No tellin'. They roam far. I saw it once. It was dusktime about two miles from here."

"Do they roam as far as Ridgeford?"

"Further, maybe."

Mr. Morton asked more questions of Sam
Goshen, but when he began to ramble, he told
him to sit down, and called upon the Indian. The
Indian, whose name was Jim Mountain, testified
that he had seen the bat and wanted to kill it, but
that I had prevented him. He made up a long
story about how he had actually seen it while he
was camped near Ridgeford.

"Fire burning," he said. "Hot fire. Tall." He
held his hands high, over his head. "Bat fly in fire.
Through fire like nothing."

The wind had died down a little, but I could
hear the stir of dry cornstalks. To the east the
purple clouds had moved closer.

Two other people were called by Mr. Morton,
a woman and an old man. Both of them had seen
the white bat flying at dusk. "Looked scary," the
woman said. "It was white with a pink mouth."
The old man had seen it three times, in the same
evening that three people died.

Mr. Morton asked then if there was anyone
who wished to testify in my behalf.

"I will," Isaac said and went over and stood in
front of him. They looked at each other as if they
had never met before in this life.

Mr. Cavendish was not listening. He was reading from a ledger he held in his lap. But the other
men seated against the wall had their eyes fixed

upon me. The faces of two of them were not un-kindly, but quizzical as though they had not made up their minds. The faces of the other two were grim, dead set against me.

I looked away, out at the fields and the blue sky. I tried to pretend to myself that I was back on Long Pond, alone in the dugout, that geese were flying and swallows were making their nests and deer were grazing in the meadows. I couldn't. All I could see was Mr. Morton standing in front of me on his short, fat legs, mean-faced and un-bending. I felt like fleeing, but I could not find the strength.

40

The curtains were flapping again as Isaac started to speak and there was thunder far off in the east. One of the men sitting against the wall said he couldn't hear very well. Isaac raised his voice.

"This meeting is outside the law," he said. "As each of you — Seth Adams, Harold Stokes, Lem Baumgarden, David Smalley, our host, Mr. Charles Cavendish, and my father, Thomas L. Morton — as you all well know, you have no authority to set a fine, impose a sentence, or carry one out should it be imposed."

Mr. Morton was standing no more than two short paces from his son, but he was not listening. He was squinting at me with a look of pure hatred.

"What you six men *can* do," Isaac said, "is to drive an innocent girl from her home. Not by means that are humane or legal, but only by means that are evil. If you do so, you are a set of fools and God will punish you."

He opened the Bible and read, " 'Judge not, that ye be not judged. For with what judgment ye judge, ye shall be judged: and with what measure ye mete, it shall be measured to you again.' "

Two of the men got up while he was talking and went to a window. They glanced out at the darkening sky and came back to report that a storm was building. The other three went and looked out. Then the first two got up again and joined the others at the window. Now no one was listening to Isaac.

It made me angry. I was tempted to use the musket.

Isaac's father hadn't moved. He stood with his feet thrust apart and his head thrown back, looking at me. I acted as if I didn't see him.

The clouds must have moved fast, because suddenly the room grew dim. There was a flash of lightning, and thunder rumbled over the roof. All of the men ran outside. I could hear their excited voices in the street, but Mr. Morton still stood there, as if he were in a trance.

The room was quiet. The wind had ceased and

the curtains had stopped flapping. Isaac opened the Bible. He waited until Mr. Morton turned his gaze from me, and their eyes met. Then he continued to read from Matthew.

There was the sound of raindrops on the roof, a dry sound, like pebbles falling. Isaac's father grew pale. Suddenly he raised his hands and let out a moan of thanksgiving.

Then he said, grasping Isaac by the shirt front. "You see, you see, we have brought the witch to justice. Now sweet rain falls upon us."

Another flash of lightning lit the room, thunder rolled, and the wind came up and blew the curtains straight out. Mr. Morton ran down the stairs. I heard him shouting. Thunder rolled again and trailed away. The post rider galloped down the street, tethered his horse at the hitching rack, and ducked inside the tavern.

It rained for only a few minutes. Then the rain stopped and the sun came out bright and hot. There was the sound of cornstalks rustling in the wind.

The men trooped silently up the stairs. Their clothes were damp from the shower. Mr. Morton took off his glasses and wiped them with a handkerchief. The post rider came in carrying the mail. He was spotted with rain and grime. Mr. Cavendish instructed a servant to bring him a drink. When it came, the rider swallowed it in one gulp and opened his pouch, which had two letters for Mr. Cavendish.

"The cost is one dollar," the post rider said.

"Fifty apiece?" Mr. Cavendish searched in his pockets and brought out a Continental bill. "One dollar. That's dear, young man."

The rider waved the bill away. "Hard cash, sir."

Mr. Cavendish went off to get the money and when he returned Isaac spoke to his father.

"A short while ago thee bragged that a witch had been brought to justice and thus 'sweet rain falls upon us.' I use thy exact words, sir. What does thee say now that the storm clouds passed over and have only spit upon the village of Ridgeford?"

Mr. Morton pounded a small fist on the billiard table. "More than ever, she's a witch."

Isaac started to answer. He paused and turned to the post rider.

"Has thee come directly down from Boston, as is thy wont?" he asked.

"Departed Boston town nine days ago," the rider replied.

"Tell me, what was the weather when thee left Boston?"

"Dry."

"Very dry?"

"Dry as a year-old codfish. Not a drop of rain

in weeks. People complain of it bitterly and pray on their knees."

"Did you find sickness along the way?"

"Sickness everywhere. Real bad in Hartford."

The rider finished his drink and closed the mail pouch. He left with a wave of a hand, ran down the stairs, and slammed the front door behind him. The clop, clop of hoofs sounded in a room that had grown quiet. Isaac glanced at the men huddled around the table.

"It is possible that bats can fly from Lake Waccabuc as far as Ridgeford village," he said. "But they cannot fly hundreds of miles to the city of Boston." He looked at each man in turn. "Is there anyone here who seriously believes otherwise?"

His father mumbled something, but fell silent. The others were silent, too. Mr. Cavendish opened his letter and began to read.

"Furthermore," Isaac said, "if the weather in Boston is dry as a year-old cod, if sickness lingers in all towns and cities and villages, then they cannot be caused by the girl who stands before you in this room."

"Witches fly," his father answered. "Around the world, if they are so minded."

Mr. Cavendish looked up from his letter. "That I doubt," he said and went on reading.

One of the men said that he likewise had doubts. Another started to say something, but coughed instead. They both looked shamefaced. Sam Goshen rose and went to a window and looked out. The Indian finished what the post rider had left in the glass.

Isaac said, "Sarah, let the men ponder on God's admonitions. It is time they did."

He took my arm and led the way down the stairs and into the ladies' parlor. He ordered two vanilla squibs and some tarts. They came on a pewter tray as Goshen and the Indian and four men of the committee trooped silently down the stairs. Mr. Morton lagged behind. When he passed the parlor he glanced in and hesitated. For a moment I thought he was about to confront me again. But he quickly turned away and stamped out into the rain-pocked street.

"My father," Isaac said, "has not changed his mind an inch. He still thinks thee is a witch and will think so until his dying day. Likewise, the apothecary, Harold Stokes. However, they are only two men against four. Father will therefore hold his tongue and not condemn thee to the village."

"I will not leave Long Pond," I said, "even if they all condemn me."

41

Through the open window came a gust of wind. People were still wandering around in the street, looking up at an empty sky.

We drank the squibs and ate the tarts, which Isaac thought were very tasteful. At least, he said they were. It was so hot that the sugar had melted on them. I didn't tell him that I myself had made the tarts the night before.

There was a sudden, distant roll of thunder. But nearer, from somewhere down the street, came the sound of hoofs. A solitary horseman rode up and stopped in front of the tavern. He was a Hessian, with long hair and a wide mustache dyed black.

He tethered his horse and hurried up the stairs and into the tavern. He glanced through the door, first at Isaac, then at me. I returned the gaze.

He went to the board at the end of the hallway. I watched him as he put up a notice. In a few minutes he was back on his horse, galloping down the street. Isaac waited for me to go out and read the notice that the Hessian had left. I didn't move.

My musket stood in the corner. Isaac glanced at it now. He smiled. "The first time I've seen thee without it. Thee must have felt brave when thee set it there. I was glad thee did not take it up when the soldier came. I wonder about the musket. When did thee get so wedded to it?"

"A long time ago. Last year. I bought it from a ferryman on the Sound. He taught me how to use it. That was after my father was killed and my brother died. When I tore a page from the Bible."

Isaac was eating a tart. He stopped eating.

"The Sermon on the Mount," I explained. "The part that says, 'Whosoever shall smite thee on thy right cheek, turn to him the other also.'"

Isaac was shocked. "Thee tore it from the Bible? Thee destroyed a page from the Holy Bible?"

"Yes, I threw it in the fire."

Isaac stared at me in disbelief. "Thee reads a Bible that has its heart torn out?"

"I don't read the Bible much."

"When thee does?"

"The Old Testament is the part I read."

"An eye for an eye and a tooth for a tooth?"

I nodded and handed him the last tart on the tray. He put it on the table and brought forth his Bible and slowly opened it to Matthew. Then with great care he tore out a single page. He held it up.

"Will thee place this in thy Bible?" he said.

"Yes."

"Will thee read it?"

"I may."

The hot breeze rustled the page.

"Pledge me that thee will," he said.

I took the page and put it in my bodice.

A clock struck the hour. Isaac jumped to his feet. "I am late to tend the store. I will be there this evening, too. Does thee require anything . . .?"

I required many things, but had no money to pay for them. "Nothing," I said.

"There is another Meeting two Sundays hence," Isaac said. "Can thee come?"

"I think so."

"Do! And bring the Bible with the page from Matthew that I have given thee. We cannot live without God's love. And our own love, which we must share with Him and with each other."

We said good-bye and he ran down the stairs and up the street. I watched him go. Mr. Cavendish was reading the notice the Hessian had posted. I was tempted to read it, too, but I left and went on my way.

The last of the sun shone through the trees on the village street. I had the musket on my shoulder. I held it tightly, for my hand was not yet healed.

My way led through a stream bed that was dry except for a mossy pool. Drinking at the pool was a snake. At the sound of my footsteps it stopped drinking. By the brown and yellow bands I recognized it as a copperhead.

The serpent lay only two short strides away. It did not try to move, but raised its head, flicked its black tongue at me, and stared with yellow eyes. I stopped and put the musket to my shoulder and took careful aim.

I was about to press the trigger when the serpent began to drink again. I watched it sip the mossy water. Then, putting the musket under my arm, I made a wide circle around the pool and went on.

Dusk came as I reached the western ridge. I looked back. Above the trees, down in the valley,

I watched the lamps in Ridgeford village go on. It was a pretty sight, to see them light up one by one. I had forgotten how pretty friendly lights could be.

About the Author

Scott O'Dell was born and grew up in Los Angeles, where he lived for many years. After college, he was a cameraman on the second company of the original motion picture of *Ben Hur*. He was with the air force in Texas during World War II and then became a book editor for a Los Angeles newspaper. For the past twenty years, he has spent his time writing books for children and adults. One of his books has won the Newbery Medal and three others were Newbery Honor Books. In addition, he is a winner of the deGrummond and Regina medals and is a recipient of the Hans Christian Andersen Author Medal, the highest international recognition for a body of work by an author of children's books. Scott O'Dell now lives in Westchester County, New York.

Books chosen with you in mind from

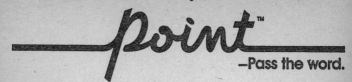

—Pass the word.

Living...loving...growing.
That's what **POINT** books are all about!
They're books you'll love reading and
will want to tell your friends about.

Don't miss these other exciting **Point** titles!

NEW POINT TITLES! $2.25 each